PLOTS, CLOTS and CALAMITY

Being Captain Cook's **TRUE** Account of H.M.S. *Endeavour* and Her Crew in the Antipodes 1770

Mark McKirdy

Copyright © 2021 by Mark McKirdy

All rights reserved.

ISBN: 978-0-6452201-0-0

Table of Contents

Introduction v

Ebb and Flow April 1770 1

Changing Currents May 1770 77

Washed Up June 1770 146

A Plot Writ Large 175

Introduction

The remarkable document revealed for the first time within these bindings began its own voyage into the broad, and sometimes hostile, waters of scholastic scrutiny and public interest on a blustery English day in the autumn of 2016. I was in residence at Balliol College, Oxford, preparing a post-doctoral dissertation on electromagnetic radiation and how microwaves in their various lengths have greatly advanced the science of reheating left-overs. As I was about to place a portion of last week's pork pie into the oven, my concentration was interrupted by a knock on the door. Upon opening it, I was greeted by a grey-haired, leather-faced old man in a blue duffel coat. When he removed the pipe from his mouth and said, "Mornin', Sir. I be William Abernathy, retired seaman, active pisspot, Sir," his voice was the deeply resonating result of years of salt, aromatic Amphora and rum. Abernathy knew of my work in the fields of science, anthropology, history and snack preparation, and he told me that he possessed a manuscript, penned by Captain James Cook in 1771, which might be of interest. Unaware at the time of the significance of his remark, I ushered him into the room and closed the door. For me, another was about to open.

Depositing his skeletonised frame into my chair, Abernathy then unbuttoned his coat and produced the dust-covered volume. I put my glasses on and read the title; *Plots, Clots and Calamity: Being Captain Cook's TRUE Account of H.M.S. Endeavour and Her Crew in the Antipodes 1770*. It was an exhilarating moment. After

| v

scanning the text for a few minutes, I asked Abernathy how he'd come by the manuscript and he explained that it had been in his family since it had been willed to his great-great grandfather, the publisher to whom Cook had submitted it following his 1770 antipodean voyage. According to my visitor, the manuscript, whose publication had been suppressed by the Admiralty because it reflected poorly on several prominent members of that august body, had then passed into the hands of succeeding Abernathy generations. As the present holder had no heirs, or indeed graces, judging by the way he polished off my pie, he had decided to present the journal to me, confident that I could secure its publication. Hence our meeting.

During the years since my introduction to the manuscript, much research has taken place in order to validate it and I am now in a position, after consulting extensively with England's A.J.P. Taylor, Australia's Geoffrey Blainey and the ruby-faced publican of my local watering hole, to stake my reputation on the fact that it is authentic. I have now released the Cook manuscript to public exhibition because of its intrinsic historical interest, its implications upon the body of work in anthropology and in the hope it will dramatically elevate the sub-zero state of my savings account, a condition that not even global warming will alter.

Mark McKirdy
On Sabbatical,
Beer Garden,
Ye Olde Cirrhosis Inn,
Aberdeen, Scotland.
2020.

Ebb and Flow
April 1770

'THURSDAY 19th April 1770
Never, in the history of great ocean voyages, has there been such a marked contrast between two succeeding days as there was between April the 18th and today.'

That was the final sentence of my log entry which signalled the beginning a truly remarkable period for my ship, *Endeavour*, and her crew. The 18th began as so many days had begun before it. A Kilkennyman master I'd once served under, on a vessel several years earlier, had a phrase that described it: "Jimmy, loif at sea's oither arse-aching boredom or it ain't. An' if it ain't, den you ain't at sea. Would y' be handin' me one more of dem bottles, Jimbo? Oi'm feelin' a wee bit tirsty."

It took me a while, but I finally worked out what the rum-ruined master was trying to say. There's a sameness to the tides and the oceans and days on ships that can become tiresome. The 18th was one of those. The sun rose and filled the sky, and the lack of a breeze again saw the ship's main topgallantsails empty. In response to the boatswain's barking, the hands then rose, cursing the early hour as usual, reported for muster then scrubbed the upper decks. That's stretching it a bit. It wasn't really a scrub; more like a light buff because the only thing any of those idlers ever put his back into was his reeking, salt-stiff shirt. At seven bells the hammocks were piped up, and at eight bells the crew was assembled for breakfast on the lower deck. As soon as the eating was done, the boatswain bellowed his familiar order: "The cap'n'll be 'ere any tick so get your grub-stuffing snouts out of the trough and swab these decks!"

I was already there, and the boatswain turned in surprise when I said quietly, "Bell swaggering again, Mr Gathrey? How many times do I have to tell you that a bully makes many threats but few friends. You'll find the men less resentful if you give them a little respect."

"I reckon the buffle-heads get as little as they deserve."

Given the cramped conditions, I stood as tall as I could and asked Gathrey if he was being deliberately obtuse. The boatswain's face reminded me of a navigation chart; blank at first then heavily lined as a scowl of uncertainty appeared.

"Ostube, Cap'n? What's..."

"Obtuse. It means dull; feeble-minded."

"How did you know what my question was going to be before I finished it?"

"Because I'm *not* obtuse. So I'll ask again. Are you being deliberately stupid?"

"No, Sir, not me. Nothin' deliberate 'bout it. It comes natural like."

"I feared as much. Gathrey, in a word, you're as thick as a blood clot."

Gathrey's thin lips formed into an irritating grin and he sucked some air into the decayed hole between his front teeth. "You said, 'in a word', then you called me a blood clot. I might be stupid but 'blood clot' is *two* words so who's ostube now?"

"Gathrey, you hulver-headed bastard," I warned with my fist in his face, "if you don't shut up, I'll darken your daylights! Now get on with it!"

"Yes, Sir. Right, lovely boys, you 'eard. Let's get some air down 'ere!"

Hatches were then opened, throwing light and air onto the damp and musty shawl that had settled over every sack, cask and barrel the previous night. At midday, the sun's altitude was taken by the ship's officers and then, in response to the master's report, the officer of the watch stepped across the quarter-deck, took off his hat, and advised our latitude.

"Make it twelve, Mr Hicks," I replied, formally marking the beginning of another nautical day. Eight bells was then sounded and the crew was ordered to lunch. Towards the pinkening evening the routine continued, with the crew being piped to their meal and then later to their hammocks on the lower deck where they were told to pipe down or else. The night watch was then set and the ship, its wake a silvery squiggle in the moonlight, followed the course determined. The conversation I had with my 3rd lieutenant in my cabin later that evening reflected the regularity.

"It's always the same. Yellow sun, blue sea and salt on the teeth. Sir, I've got an idea. Remember those chess games we played at the start of the voyage, the ones where we drank a couple of beers and you kicked your shoes off and talked about your family? How about a game now?"

"No thank you. I'm too preoccupied with this southern continent. If we don't find it soon we'll be forced to sail home with part of our commission incomplete, and that's not a prospect I welcome. I'd rather the ship went down with all hands."

Gore unbuttoned the collar of his shirt and shook his head. "I'm not sure the hands would feel the same sense of duty, given that they're all devout quakers."

"Quakers? Who told you that load of rubbish?"

"Nobody. I've seen them. Quaking in their boots when it's rough, trembling in their hammocks in the dark. There aren't enough vertebrae between the lot of them to make a complete backbone."

For once, Gore was right. Even though he'd come to the *Endeavour* with an enviable reputation, I concluded very early in the voyage that the only types likely to envy John Gore's standing were those involved with selling either pest-infested property or used carriages. But he did have a quality which I found attractive; he consistently proved himself to be the quintessential dormedory who made himself scarce on just about every occasion involving work or decisions. It was a case of out of sight, out of mind; my sight, his mind.

"John," I said, mesmerised by the scene of his long fingers scratching at the chatts leaping through his oily, carrot-cropped hair, "you're quick to point out the speck in your brother's eye, but you should take a look at yourself now and then. You might see the log in your own."

Gore had trouble grappling with the gist of the comment. "How would a log get in my eye in the first..."

"Don't bother closing the door when you leave. I'll do it."

I did, and the hull, decks, masts and rigging all vibrated for a solid minute. It had been just another twenty-four hours in a twenty-four-month voyage, and with the words 'New day, new land' recited in unison with the rhythm of the tick-tocking clock in the cabin, I lay on my bed and stared through the porthole. A shooting star flared across the sky, its light-line impressed on my retinas as my eyes closed. It was just past 2 a.m..

Then at dawn on the 19th, as six bells was sounding and the ship's bow was slicing through a paper-smooth sea under a southern sky that was just beginning to flame with new energy and hope, I was woken by a startling cry from the masthead lookout that echoed long and loud through every part of the ship;

"I'M SCARED OF FUCKIN' HEIGHTS!"

A melancholic sigh escaped from my core as I threw back the blanket. But then it happened; a second shout, more urgent than the first, heralding that our half-penny days had passed and a wealth of new experiences was about to begin;

"LAND FUCKIN' HO! *NOW* CAN I CLIMB DOWN?"

It was the cry that I'd been waiting weeks to hear. As I pulled on my uniform and opened the cabin door, a melee of marines was rushing past.

"Mornin', Cap'n!"

"Good news, eh, Skipper?"

"Comin' up. Sir? Sounds like we've done it! The Great Southern Continent! Let's hope it's not another Nieuw Zeeland."

"Look out, you bastards! I'm comin' through like one of the cook's oat cakes! Oh, sorry, Sir, didn't see you there. After you."

I told Sergeant Edgecumbe to lower his voice and move his carcass out of the way. As I stepped into the narrow corridor, surrounded by bright smiles, blackened teeth and stubbled chins, my mind flashed back to the last port of call just mentioned by the charging seaman. It was the island group Abel Tasman first called 'Staten Landt' in 1642, and while I'd relished the six-month challenge of charting its coast and recording some observations regarding the war-like, tattooed natives, there wasn't much else of note. The bubbling mud held little scientific significance and I agreed, at least in part, with Joseph Banks when he'd said one day ashore, "Mr Cook, warm springs are only worth jumping into when they're supporting a feathered mattress. And a feathered mattress is only worth jumping onto when it's supporting some giggling country maiden with large holdings. Know what I mean?"

I knew precisely what the indulged lecher had meant but I didn't bother commenting. In fact, a lot of Joseph's conversation during the three years wasn't worth commenting on. He was in some respects like Nieuw Zeeland. The most attractive part of one was its rapidly receding shoreline and the most gratifying part of the other was his steadily receding hairline.

So on this invigorating April morning, with the wind in my face and a speckling of salt on my lips, I stood on the *Endeavour's* quarter-deck and viewed the object of our search for the first time. And what a remarkable sight it was. Truly exceptional. From a distance of almost a league, the land appeared to be rather flat and brownish-green, with almost no hills as interruptions. A few trees, similar in size to poplars and with thick canopies, were scattered at irregular intervals, their dark green foliage contrasted by the white feathers of the birds that flocked and squawked all about them.

Surrounding these trees, for as far as the eye could see, was a low, woody scrub. They reminded me of guardsmen in busbies encircled by a crowd of scruffy-haired East London urchins. Through the telescope, there was no sign of any natives, although several crude shelters and the remnants of as many cooking fires were visible near a clearing at the shore. It was this shore which really commanded one's attention. Wide and white as a tablecloth, flattened even more by the occasional breaker that swept on to it and then swept quickly back. I closed my eyes for a couple of seconds, breathed deeply and then opened them. To my eternal relief, the land was still there. On the quarter-deck with me were John Gore, 2nd Lieutenant Hicks, Joseph Banks and his two dogs carried from England.

"Anybody want a hug?" the wide-eyed 2nd lieutenant said to no one in particular. "One minute you're dragging yourself around the ship with your arse out of your breeches, and bingo, the next sees you up here pissing yourself with excitement."

None of us dared move so much as an eyelash, let alone an embracing arm. It was the sort of comment I'd heard often from Zachariah, a lanky man whose spirit and substance depended for their happiness upon one factor - the sea. From it flowed his joy and purpose, and his knowledge of it, according to him, was an indispensable addition to my own. Again by his own assessment, he was competent, mature and hesitant to defer to lesser intellects. Gore's judgement was slightly different, and I'll quote the words he used in his speech of welcome in the officers' mess not long after we'd sailed from England: "Mr Hicks, I know I speak for the entire British navy when I say you're the sort of officer who brings cheer to his shipmates the minute you take your leave."

"Hear hear!" chorused his shipmates as he flung the door open and stormed out.

So when the first glimpse of the Great Southern Continent was acknowledged with shouts and acclamation from Mr Banks, my chest heaved. Mr Gore's chest was also heaving, but it had less to do with pride and more to do with the swells we were riding. "You don't seem your normal chirpy self, John," Hicks commented. "This is a moment that will go down in history so perk up."

Gore's literal interpretation of the suggestion sent several crewmen scurrying for cover. Not so mobile was the ship's goat, the one which had previously circumnavigated the globe with Samuel Wallis in his ship, *Dolphin*. It was a reliable milker, essential for our coffee, and it had been kept atop since leaving Nieuw Zeeland because the smell below had become intolerable. For the goat, that is, so to get it away from the reek of the ranks, I had it tethered to the windlass. Now here it was, being banged and buffeted by panic-driven sailors, its hooves slipping and eyes bulging as it spun in ever-diminishing circles. Finally the rope gave way under the strain and the enraged ruminant made a direct charge towards the only part of Gore which wasn't hanging over the quarter-deck's rail. And at the eagerly anticipated moment when horns were just about to contact hindquarters, Gore straightened and stepped aside. Undeterred, the bleating, blurting goat kept going, ramming the rail and knocking itself stupid.

"That's better," Gore said as he wiped his mouth with his sleeve. "I feel like a new man."

Sergeant Edgecumbe stepped out from behind the main mast and hoisted the goat onto his broad shoulders.

"You won't find any up here, Mr Gore," he said, slipping slightly on the wet deck, "but I'll see if I can get you one below after I've dumped this poor bugger in the hold."

As was his want, Joseph Banks then sought to impose himself into the situation. "Mr Cook," he announced, steadying himself by grabbing hold of the rigging, "I suggest we pay no further mind to the goat and concentrate our intellects upon the imperatives of nomenclature which will elevate an already distinguished member of our company to a pre-destined, socio-historical prominence; a stature iconic in its influence and..."

My jaw clenched involuntarily. "Will you speak plainly! You're not at a Royal Society meeting now!"

"All right," he snapped, gazing towards the shore. "Because that outcropping of rugged land is over there and I'm here, I propose that it be called *Cape Banks*. Be a good chap, James, and jot that down on the chart".

Enraged by his insolence and self-importance, I told him, in no uncertain terms, that I wasn't one of his Lincolnshire servants employed for the sole purpose of toadying to his privileged conceits. Before he had a chance to respond, I asked the others to suggest alternative names. 2nd Lieutenant Hicks wasted no time in adding his tuppenceworth of grey-matter. "I vote we call it *Point Hicks*."

"*Point Hicks* be damned!" Banks bellowed. "I'm the eminent scientist. What are you? A working-class waste of skin in a silly hat."

Overhead, a lone gull hovered against the breeze as Hicks stood his ground. "I say it should be called *Point Hicks* because I was the first to point at it."

Hicks may have been a waste of skin, but because we shared the same stature in society, and similarly styled hats, Banks had as much chance as clean sheets in a shagging-shop.

"Sounds fine to me," I said. "What about you, Mr Gore? Any objections?"

Gore had his backside upside and his head over the rail again. I swallowed hard and stepped back just as a thundering, chundering gurgle rent the air. "Was that a *no*? Good, that's settled. *Point Hicks* it is."

Incensed by the rebuff, Banks' face turned a furious red and the large vein in his forehead bulged. He then seized his whippets, thumped Gore in the guts for good measure and strutted off to his cabin. I was not surprised by his churlishness because he was simply displaying the two characteristics common to all men of upper-class position; a thick head and a thin skin.

At the time, the incident struck me as being trivial, so I didn't attempt to call Banks back. Hicks took a different view, which was nothing new. "You'd better say something to him, Captain, or you know what'll happen. He'll sit in his cabin and sulk and hate us even more because we're the type who work for wages. Toffs are like that. I reckon those notions come with their mothers' milk."

Gore came up for air, heard the word *milk* and then went down again. I looked at my hands as they gripped the rail. The knuckles were white. "As far as I'm concerned, the arrogant little bedbug can stuff himself into one of his jars, jam the stopper and rot in his cabin forever."

Hicks' eye-brows shot up as he asked why my language was less tempered than usual. My hands tightened even more. "Because the effect is quicker than grog and less guilt-ridden than murder. Does that answer your bloody idiotic question?"

The lieutenant nodded, then added obsequiously, "And you're right about Banks. Let the stupid little prick sulk till the cows come home. Who frigging-well cares?"

"If you mention cows or milk again, Zachariah," Gore spluttered, turning seaweed green as he dropped to the deck, "I'll kick your arse so hard it'll be flatter than your head and uglier than your face!"

As I took the wheel, I heard myself laughing for the first time in months.

Although I didn't ever tell him, I realised later that Hicks had been right and that I should have said something to Banks. Here, in a distant latitude and adjacent to an uncertain shore, my prejudice had unwittingly sown the seeds of disharmony which were to bear much soured fruit during the remainder of our southern voyage.

To set the record straight, just so that I can sleep without waking in a cold sweat, I want to reveal, for the first time, that it was this disharmony which almost ended our journey and our lives on the coral reef near *Cape Tribulation* two months and 1,650 miles further on. I am fully aware that this contradicts my official journal, in which I stated that the reason for our running aground on the reef was the inconstancy of unfamiliar waters. The waters were a factor but only a minor one.

This revelation may well cause the Admiralty to review my status and naval future. If so, then it's a price I'm willing to pay because the worry bound up in half-truth is becoming unbearable. And it's worse when

Elizabeth and I fight. At any given moment, the slightest glance is enough to provoke an argument, one I can never win. "You're a father," she says at the end, "so for your children's sake, tell what really happened." A knife in the heart.

And when we're not bickering, we simply sit in the cold silence of our separation and loathe both the distance and the deception. She's not the same woman she was three years ago and I haven't got a clue why. All I know is that since returning from the voyage, the Elizabeth Batts whom I married in the Parish Church of Little Barking ten years ago is now a terrier yapping at my heels. It has to stop.

So, a short time after land had been sighted and Banks had taken himself below, he clambered up through the main hatch and joined Hicks and me at the wheel. I'd hoped that his earlier outburst would have caused him to be a little embarrassed, but when he smiled, held out his arms and shouted, "I'm back, chaps, but please don't cheer!", I sensed that the botanist's lexicon didn't list the term *shrinking violet*. Wanting no further strife, I welcomed him with a casual nod and then asked him to identify certain structures which dotted the shoreline and distant hills. Joseph pondered for a moment or two, then, without asking if he could borrow it, grabbed my telescope and clamped it to his eye. He then dropped the 'scope onto the deck and called for one of his reference books. It was brought by Briscoe, one of his retainers, and after his master had consulted several pages, he looked up and announced, "According to this, they're trees of some sort."

In order to minimise the irritation which my twitching fingers betrayed, I then mentioned to Zachariah my curiosity regarding some smoke billowing near the beach. The 2nd lieutenant immediately conferred with Banks, turned back to me as I picked up the 'scope and said, "He tells me it's the visible vapour from burning substances." In terms of a heroic act of will, it didn't take much to ignore Hicks.

"Joseph," I said as I turned the wheel gently, "where were you educated?"

"At Harrow and Eton and then Oxford."

The ship listed slightly to port, crested a wave and then levelled. "And you were made a member of the Royal Society at what... twenty-eight?"

"It was twenty-two. The youngest to be given such an honour and damned-well deserved, I might add."

"I thought you might. And roughly how much do your estates in Lincolnshire, Derbyshire and Sussex bring in each year?"

Banks uncurled eight plump, lily-white fingers. "About six thousand pounds."

"And you're on good terms with the Earl of Sandwich and King George?"

"Absolutely. But what's all this leading to?"

"Well, Joseph, it's like this. You've got wealth, education, prominent connections and prestige, so why am I convinced that you're a congenital nigmenog?"

Banks grabbed the wheel, held it rock steady and looked me straight in the eyes. "Just who are you calling stupid?"

I answered by simply returning his stare. With that, the botanist turned on his heels and was gone again.

When Hicks saw me rubbing the backs of my aching legs, he took control of the ship's course and said, "Good on you. I bet nobody's had the courage to call him stupid before."

A large swell suddenly caused me to grab hold of the poop's rail. "Perhaps, but I believe in speaking it as I see it. By the way, has anyone bothered to wash this rail down since Gore puked on it?"

Like some pesty mole coming up for air. Banks' head popped up through the hatch. "*Now* who's the nigmenog, Mr Cook?"

Again my knuckles turned white, in fairly definite contrast to the little bits of orange, green and pink muck that oozed up between them. A four-letter word expanded in my throat then exploded across the blue, brine-brimming valleys. "GORE!"

Wisely, Zachariah took a step back. "You're not happy, are you?"

As the sun vanished behind a fleecy cloud, I took a small step towards the 2nd lieutenant, who in turn took a lamb-white leap in the direction of the main hatch.

"And you're sharp as a tack-head. See the hatch? Open it. See the hole? Fill it now! Boatswain, drag yourself up here and take the wheel!"

What on earth had happened to this day that had promised so much? There had been times in the voyage, admittedly few, when I'd enjoyed the smells of cabbage, wet wood and livestock which filled every hold and cabin. The stench now was overwhelming. Once the flap of a sail or the slap of water against the bow was a sound that rang in my ears like the bells of some great cathedral.

I listened, and now all I could hear were fingernails desperately scratching down a prison wall. I went below to my suite, opened the Bible, and read about the trials of Job. After twenty minutes or so, I was convinced that in relative terms, he had little to grizzle about. As I closed the book and settled back into the sighing leather of the chair, my father's words came quietly into my thoughts. 'James,' he would say to me as a lad all those years ago, 'thou'll get nowt in life by sittin' and thinkin'. Doin' is what brings in the crops. Little by little and the job's soon done. Lad, thou can't sit on thy hands frettin' if they've got a dirty big shovel in 'em and a pile o' earth to be moved'.

It was time to shift some sods, and the carpenter was going to be first. I stood and opened the porthole. Air flooded in, fresh and full. Grabbing hold of the door's cold, brass knob with both hands, I twisted, pulled the door open and stepped outside. In the dim, yellow lamp-light, I made my way down to the carpenters' storeroom aft on the lower deck, thumped on the door and entered. John Satterley was on the floor, recumbent and snoring like a congested porker, so I wrenched off his wooden leg and pounded the planks near his head.

"What the fuc..." he shouted as he jumped to his foot. "Oh, it's you, Cap'n. Blimey, you're a sight for sore eyes. I don't get many visitors down 'ere."

"No wonder. That sign on your door that says 'PISS OFF!' isn't much of an encouragement to anyone. Pull it down."

"I can't. The hinges are on real solid."

"Not the *door*, the sign."

"What! And 'ave the likes of Hicks an' Gore hangin' around like smells in a privy. Not on your nelly! So what's up? I'm terrible busy at the moment."

While I had been thinking in my cabin, an idea had struck. Why not give the men an opportunity to express their grievances? If they knew they had a say in the day-to-day running of the ship, it seemed likely that strife would be reduced.

"Mr Satterley, I want you to construct a box. Not too big, mind. About the size of that thing over there you keep your nails in. It's to be completely sealed except for a slot at the top. You've got half an hour to finish it then bring it to my cabin. And get rid of the sign now. "

Thirty minutes later Satterley brought the box up. I was discussing my idea with Lieutenant Hicks over coffee and he was in agreement.

"The notion's good, Captain. If we encourage the men to jot down their ideas and concerns and then put them in the box, I'm positive they'll all be a lot happier. And it'll certainly put to rest some of the negative feelings towards you."

I asked him to be more specific.

"Some of the lads think all your years at sea have turned you a bit crusty and short-tempered."

"That's rubbish," I snapped as I dropped my cup back onto its saucer. "I was short-tempered long before I joined the navy."

"That's what I told them. I also said that appearances can be misleading and that beneath your stiff jacket there beats a heart..."

"Yes, go on, a heart of...?"

"Nothing, just a heart. Some of them think you don't have one at all."

"So that's your idea of support? Now, about the box. Any other thoughts?"

Hicks pensively ran his finger around the rim of his cup and nodded. I poured my usual second cup, added exactly one level teaspoon of sugar and told the lieutenant to speak his piece.

"I don't think many of the ninnyhammers can read and write."

After a moment's deliberation, I came up with the suggestion that any illiterates could sketch their ideas.

"Splendid," the lieutenant gushed. "It's obvious why the Admiralty chose you to lead this expedition."

The soft-soaping was being applied a little too thickly for my liking, so I told Hicks to confine it to the ablutions area. I then ordered him to assemble the men on the main deck because I wanted to tell them about the box.

A few minutes later I could hear Hicks yelling "All hands on deck!", so I waited the appropriate time then strode up. As I climbed through the hatch, the sun flared like a match in a cave, blinding me for a moment. It was strong, brilliant, and our English light seemed spiritless in comparison. A mile or so to port, the land was a ribbon of rippling green, and under the ship, the sea groaned its depth and weight as it rolled gently over. A cormorant settled on the spritsail-yard, spearing its hungry gaze into the water. Then, like a dart, it went down, skewered its silvery catch and quickly flew off. I followed its flight, looking for the horizon but unable to make it out against the sweep and reach of blue, pacific sky.

The voice that steadily bored into my ear was like some small, irritating insect. "Captain, did you hear me... the crew's waiting... Sir?"

I had heard him. Even in my sleep I heard him. "All right, Hicks. Now stand behind me, shut your potato trap and give your red rag a rest. Men," I continued, lifting the box up and casting my eyes over the lines of curious brown faces that swamped the deck, "can anyone tell me what this is?"

Nobody answered, so I lifted the box higher. From the back of the ranks an arm waved frantically.

"Yes, Able Seaman Peckover?"

"Beggin' the Cap'n's pardon, Cap'n, Sir, but it be your hand, Cap'n, Sir."

The sun grew a little less radiant.

"You're a simpleton, Peckover," Hicks ventured over my shoulder.

"Why, thank you, Mr 'icks. Only too glad to be of 'elp."

I got straight to the point. "Lads, if anyone's giving you trouble, or if you can think of a way to make things run more happily, jot it down and put it in this box. And if you can't write, then sketch your suggestion. The best idea will be awarded a monthly prize. And you needn't be afraid to speak plainly because you don't have to sign your name. Are there any questions?"

Peckover's hand went up again. "Beggin' the Cap'n's pardon, but if you don't want us to be signin' our name, 'ow will you know who wins the monthly prize?"

Hicks' mouth was quickly at my ear. "Peckover's right."

I reluctantly agreed, advised the men that they could sign their names then asked if anyone else had a question.

Peckover persisted. "But what if some bilge rat writes an 'orrible comment about an officer and then signs someone else's name? Will the wrong man be flogged?"

My jaw tightened involuntarily. "You answer him, Mr Hicks. I've lost patience."

Hicks stepped forward of the quarter-deck, stood beside me and said, "To avoid the possibility of that happening, I order that no names whatsoever be signed. But you can if you want to. Now if there are no more...?"

"Just one, Mr 'icks."

"Bugger me, Peckover! What is it this time?"

"What be the monthly prize?"

Before the furious lieutenant could charge into the ranks to throttle the seaman, I pre-emptively seized his salt-stiff collar and said, "Stand there and listen. You might learn something. Men, this is an opportunity for you all to begin participating in the scheme. You're going to decide the prize. Mr Hicks, hand out pencils and paper. When the boatswain presents you with the box, lads, put your paper into it. We'll adopt the most popular suggestion."

When the last paper had been inserted, the boatswain squeezed his bulk through the ranks, around the masts and brought me the box. And it was then that I saw the problem. There was a slot but no lid so the wretched thing couldn't be opened. At least not by the usual method. Down to the deck dropped the varnished container and down went my polished boot on top of it. Toe, heel, sole, the lot. All thumping and grinding.

"Don't worry, men," I said, glowering at Satterley, "this was only a replica. From this evening you'll find the proper box nailed to the wall outside my cabin. Now, let's hear what you've all had to say. Stand easy while Mr Hicks reads out the first suggestion."

Hicks picked through the splinters and seized a crumpled piece of paper. He smoothed it out and glanced at the writing. "You wouldn't be interested in this one. I'll just grab another one."

"Lieutenant, everyone's ideas, no matter how trivial, are of equal interest so read what's there!"

Hicks stood chastened. "Sorry. It says here 'I vote we troll for sharks using Hicks as bait. Yours truly, J. Gore'. "

The sun suddenly went dark and another headache was coming on.

"Next one, Lieutenant."

"Let's see... 'a night in bed with the wife. And I don't care whose wife. J. Banks, Esq.' And there's a sort of stick-drawing with it, like the ones kids do. It shows a woman and a bloke with his Long Johns round his ankles and she's all goggle-eyed because..."

"That's enough. Boatswain, dismiss the men!"

After a while the sound of running feet died away, and in its place came the susurration of wind through sails. It was as if each caress of the canvas was somehow extending down to me. An odd, unexpected experience, but nonetheless real. It also brought with it a clarity of thought; an absolute determination to press on. Even though the initial experiment with the box had been unsuccessful, there was every reason to persevere. Much depended on its acceptance.

So I went back to the carpenters' storeroom and ordered Satterley to construct a new box. "And make sure I don't have to use my bloody boot to open it!" I then stipulated that I wanted it nailed to the wall outside my cabin by night-fall. Two hours later Satterley was humming and hammering on the wall.

"It's up, Cap'n," he shouted. "Come and look."

There it was, square, smooth and varnished, with a neat slot and its own boot attached.

I immediately ordered the carpenter inside, so he hopped in and supported himself on my desk. He coughed, twitched then scratched his beard. A few drops of perspiration formed on his forehead.

"John," I said, "just so that you know where you stand, let me spell it out. I want a box with a lid; l for loggerhead, i for idiot, d for dimarse. Lid. Now piss off and do it properly!"

Had the box been in place at the time I'd wanted, the friction that continued during the remainder of April might well have been minimised. Two crewmen in particular were central to the disharmony, and the incident involving the normally placid Master Robert Molyneux and his mate, Richard Pickersgill, on the evening of the 21st, came as something of a shock. Although neither was particularly bright, they'd performed with average competence and kept themselves out of trouble. So it was my guess that the boredom of routine and the close proximity to rising tensions within others must have had a deleterious effect.

Molyneux was big and gruff with hair like a wheat field in a hurricane. There was no doubt that his brain had been addled through frequent handshakes with the bottle in just about every ale-house in Europe, but to his credit, he at least answered to the correct name at muster. That made him fairly unique, because most of the men were so used to using aliases that at the start of the voyage, muster had been a parade of either the shameless, nameless, infamous or bogus. I recall that on the second morning out of England, several of the crew, keen to keep their names away from the public ear, had substituted the issued roll with a fraud. As a result, the boatswain conducted muster something along these lines:

"Able Seaman Anderson?"
"Yes, Boatswain."
"Able Seaman the Great, Alexander?"
"Aye aye."
"Gunner Bowles?"
"Here."
"Gunner Arc, Joan of?"
"The voices, the voices, they're drivin' me mad."
"Master Molyneux?"
"Sir."
"Master's Mate Newton, Sir Isaac?"
"Aye."
"Sailmaker Pope Paul 1V?"
"Bless you, me old son."
"Carpenter Satterley?"
"Piss off!"
"Carpenter's Mate Columbus, Christopher?"
"Vete a la mierda!"

When I sought to discover who had initiated the scheme, Molyneux was quick to point the finger at his mate, Pickersgill. It was from that moment that the relationship between the two soured. Like Molyneux, Richard Pickersgill was large. Dark-haired and granite-jawed, the young mate was generally regarded as being a loyal and skilled observer, qualities apparently not missed by Lieutenant Hicks. Not long after we'd sailed from England, he visited my suite for a chat concerning those crew members who could be trusted and those who couldn't.

The lieutenant took a note-pad from his vest pocket and began reading the accounts he had made of each of the men. He seemed a little nervous in my company so I told him to relax. He thanked me, crossed his legs and sipped at his port. It wasn't long before mild apoplexy set in. As his eyes rolled back into his head, I seized his glass and flung the contents through the window, mentally noting to speak to the Victualling Board about its source of supply in relation to this particular ration. While cheapness was an important factor, it was generally known that the sweat-shops of Manchester have never been hailed as the home of fortified wine.

As his vision cleared, Hicks paused at the account of the mate, looked up at me and said, "If there's anyone on board who won't crack under strain, it's Richard Pickersgill."

I knew at once that Pickersgill would prove to be about as useful as a cork anchor.

The evening of the 21st was typical of many during that season in those southern latitudes and it reminded me of the imitative scribblings from the Literary Editor of *The London Evening Post* - cold as a critic's text but lacking the sting that takes one's breath away.

As Lieutenant Gore and I stood on the quarter-deck, through the owl-light we noticed Molyneux and Pickersgill in animated conversation at the bow. Molyneux then pointed towards a mountain to port about half a league off. It was hump-shaped and thickly covered with trees. A whisper-thin mist haloed the apex and high above, a million stars were just beginning to shimmer on the violet blanket.

Noticing Gore and me at the stern, Molyneux ran back. Pickersgill quickly followed.

"Captain," the master blurted out, the warm air from his mouth frosting in the chill. "See that thing over there? What are the chances we call it *Mount Molyneux*?"

"About the same as the chances of you becoming next in line to the throne of France," his mate sneered. "I bloody seen it first, so it should be *Mount Pickersgill*."

"Watch your fuckin' language in front of the captain," Gore reprimanded. "You bloody *saw* it first, not seen."

Molyneux was having none of it. "He bloody didn't saw it first, he seed it second."

The conversation see-sawed like this until Gore proposed a compromise. "Why don't we name the mountain after both of you? I'll take a part of each of your last names and combine them."

"That sounds fair t' me," Molyneux said, barely able to supress the self-important grin that turned his mouth into a half-moon.

"Me, too," Pickersgill agreed as he placed his arm around the master's shoulder. "This way we'll both make it into the history books."

Although it was nippy, Gore's chest rose with the hot air of the self-important. "Then it's settled. It shall henceforth be known as *Mount Neuxspicker*."

Before I had a chance to overrule the 3rd lieutenant, Molyneux shouted, "*Mount Nosepicker!*" and kicked a slops bucket down the length of the deck and into the fore-mast. Upon hearing the crash, the boatswain dashed up through the main hatch, his eyes wide in the gloom and his voice thunderous as he asked what was happening. He then saw me and fell silent. Impressed by his deference, I said that it was just a minor misunderstanding and then tried to lessen the tension by joking that it could easily be settled by the cat and a few days in the hold.

"The cat!" the master shouted into the cold, tea-black calmness. "Well, if I'm goin' t' be flogged, I might as well give youse all a decent excuse." With that, he lunged at Pickersgill's hair and dragged out oily, brown clumps. Gore wrenched the two apart and the culprits hung their heads as the lieutenant acted to re-establish some degree of authority.

"Captain, may I suggest an alternative name for the feature? One that should placate Mr Banks' hurt feelings over your earlier refusal to name the cape after him."

"I'm listening."

"What about *Mount Dromedary*?"

The darkness hindered my vision, so I raised the 'scope, peered, then acknowledged the botanist's interest in flora and fauna.

"No, it's got nothin' to do with faulorna or whatever, does it, Mr Hicks?" Molyneux sniggered. "It's about the camel's shape... its hump... the same as what that cry baby Banks gets whenever he's offended."

Unfortunately, Joseph, who had been taking in the evening air just at that moment, overheard the master's remark and demanded an apology.

"All right," Molyneux said, "I'm sorry... that you get the hump, like what you've got now."

Pickersgill's cheeks ballooned as he tried to contain his amusement, and then finally burst as Banks slipped on the slops that had been spilt earlier. Recalling a previous encounter with the botanist, one in which I'd come off second-best, I felt like shouting, "*Now* who's the bloody nigmenog?", but it was not the time for settling old scores. I craved the satisfaction of dealing with this new one, so I immediately called for Sergeant Edgecumbe and a party of marines. Acting on my orders, the corps swiftly confined the master and his mate to the hold until the rising of the sun. Even though it was their first major offence, they needed a period of detention as punishment.

A short time later, as the 3rd lieutenant and I left the quarter-deck at the changing of the watch, Gore paused at the hatch. "Captain, so that those two hoddypeaks can show Mr Banks they're sorry about what happened, why don't we make them sit in on one of his plant lectures?"

I pushed Gore aside, clambered down through the hatch and closed it firmly on his feet. "Their crime has been given the appropriate punishment," I called through the grating. "Adding hard labour isn't justified."

Under the laws relating to life at sea, I could have had the offenders flogged, but the scars of resentment and hostility would have remained long after any physical blemish had healed. In hindsight, I should have had them beaten until they were as blue as the brine, because the following day they were at each other's throats again. It's almost impossible to imagine that a misunderstood word could have led to a fierce brawl, but that was the reason for it, as told to me by the person who'd witnessed it, Sergeant Edgecumbe. After Molyneux and his mate had been released from the hold following their detention, they went up on deck to check the hempen cable leading from the anchor to the main capstan. I'd sent Edgecumbe with them, just in case. Pickersgill noticed that a section of the cable was frayed, so he'd drawn Molyneux's attention to it. The master, still angered by the previous day's events, studied the cable and reluctantly nodded his head in agreement.

"It irks me to say this, Pickersgill," Molyneux apparently muttered, "but I agree with Lieutenant Hicks. You're alert."

Upon hearing this, young Pickersgill picked up the sodden cable and wrapped it around the master's throat. His huge, sun-bronzed hands twisted the rope till his knuckles whitened. "Don't you call me a lert!" he'd shouted. "If anyone on this ship's a friggin' lert, it's you!"

According to Edgecumbe, the half-choked master's face immediately resembled a pudding, with his eyes bulging like plums and his wet, yellow hair spreading across his forehead like custard. Fortunately, the mate was quick to come to his senses, and he released his grip. Molyneux was taking great gulps of air as Edgecumbe grabbed them both by the front of their shirts and dragged them down to my cabin.

"So there you 'ave it," the sergeant said, concluding his report. "Two grown men fightin' like dogs in a ditch."

"It wasn't my fault," Pickersgill said, his eyes arrowing into the mate. "He called me a lert."

Molyneux rubbed his throat. "Listen you idiot, I didn't say you was a lert, as in *one* lert. I said you was alert as in *awake*."

Pickersgill was quick to respond. "*Now* who's the idiot? A wake is a party for a dead geezer. Which is what you're about to become. Get out of me way, Edgecumbe! I'm goin' t' kick the bastard fair in the old testaments!"

It was as well that Edgecumbe had remained between them, for they showed all the restraint of friars at their first lunch after Lent. Banging my fists down on the desk, I stood up and pushed the chair back against the wall. For the next sixty seconds, I battered their ears with just about every Anglo-Saxon expletive I could think of. Just as my voice was becoming hoarse, I ordered the sergeant to take them up to the main deck, rip their shirts off and give each of them three strokes in front of the crew. The hope was that it would be a lesson to everyone.

My father had a saying about hopes and I've never forgotten a word of it. Even the rise and fall of his earth-deep voice. 'Lad,' he'd begin over a mug of ale in the kitchen after he'd come in from work, 'hopes are like stones. They can either be strong, endurin' foundations for a man's soul...' and here his voice would lower into a lament; close yet somehow distant... 'or they can crumble into dust and blow thy spirit fair away'. I can barely recall a day during this period at sea when the wind of failing hope wasn't howling.

However, in defence of the men, it would be unfair not to acknowledge their confinement as being in large part responsible for their dispositions. Since leaving Nieuw Zeeland, they'd been forced to live and work within an arm's distance of one another. Given the discomfort, trouble seemed inevitable.

Nieuw Zeeland had given the men some release, but because excursions ashore usually involved gathering fresh provisions or surveying, activities otherwise known as *work*, the newness soon lost its allure. Eventually there came a time when the men never left the ship, much to the annoyance of the boatswain, and only occasionally when it was actually anchored. The major problem simmering within the crew, and which was making their present confinement even more unendurable, was related to a previous port of call.

Nearly twelve months earlier we'd stayed for a period in Otaheite, that fabled group of islands discovered by Samuel Wallis in June, 1767, and I'm sure that it was the memory of this paradise, and the panting after its pleasures, that were largely responsible for the present agitation. According to Mr Gathrey, coming upon it was like '... bumpin' into an honest politician in the House of Commons or trippin' over a newspaper scribbler at nine in the mornin' who was sober enough to remember his own name; almost too bloody good to be true.'

When we first arrived, the men, made amiable by the natural grace of the natives, golden heat, moist, fertile soil, succulent fruits and turquoise lagoons with their soft sands, built a fort, repaired the long-boat and collected water and fresh provisions. Those who were capable of performing minor calculations helped the scientific party observe the Transit of Venus, while those more interested in money matters engaged themselves in trading with the natives. Given his wealth and commercial experience, Joseph Banks was the most active in this area. On one occasion a young man approached him at the gate of the fort. The young male presented a roll of cloth, a litter of hogs, two sacks of bananas, five small shrubs and a canoe. Joseph cast a dismissive glance over the lot then offered a snuff-box in return. Having dealt with the bullying botanist before, the native trader reluctantly took the trinket and then pointed in the direction of a distant female. Banks cupped his eyes and squinted in the glare, so the young trader clapped his hands and beckoned for his dusky companion to come forward. As she approached, Joseph's knees wilted. Standing no more than 30 inches from his sweating palms was a girl of exquisite beauty; long black hair, lithe brown limbs, bare breasts, chocolate-dark eyes and a smile sultry enough to melt marble.

In line with both his custom and his character, the botanist came in low. "A specimen jar?"

This time the young trader shook his head.

"I see. Then how's this... a specimen jar *and* a pressed frog?"

No response.

"All right, but this is definitely my last offer. A jar, a flat frog and my Lincolnshire estates. Take it or leave it."

A fuzzy-haired nod of acceptance closed the transaction.

At this point I intervened. While I was aware that our island hosts were accommodating with regard to certain activities, namely the *horizontal hula*, to use Joseph's colourful term, I strongly believed that to barter for affection was unworthy of anyone who called himself a gentleman. I grabbed Joseph's arm and dragged him into my tent. I then told him that trading for the delights of the flesh was contemptible and that he should give serious thought to setting a proper example to the men.

"How dare you!" he shouted. "My very presence is an example."

I looked around the tent for something solid to thump. The botanist's head was the obvious choice but I successfully fought the impulse. "Banks, your presence is an example, but it's a bloody embarrassing one! You posture from dawn till dusk and allow what's wobbling in your trousers to govern what's lolling on your shoulders."

Breathing deeply and quickly, I flung back the flap of the tent. The fragrance of frangipani drifted in, partially dissipating the bad air between us. "I need a walk," I said. "Think carefully about what you intend doing and tell me when I get back. And keep in mind that you're supposed to be an English gentleman."

As I stooped through the opening, Briscoe, Banks' retainer, came in with some papers. Five minutes later I rejoined the botanist and sat on the edge of my bunk.

"What's it to be?" The quietness that always accompanies deliberation was heavy in the tent.

"It wasn't easy," Joseph said. "I had decided to press ahead, even going so far as to sign these papers that Briscoe brought transferring ownership of my estates. But then your words about being a man of position made me realise that I had certain responsibilities. So I won't be proceeding."

I shook Banks' limp hand. "That's heartening. Well done."

As we walked outside into the enveloping heat to tell the native trader, I added further approval of Joseph's decision by reminding him that everything his father had worked for was now not going to be squandered. Like a cat after its master's canary, a knowing smile crept across the carpet of the botanist's face.

"Mr Cook," he said, shuffling through the papers, "I may be an English gentleman, but I'm not your typical *Henry Haw-Haw*. My estates were in no danger."

"But didn't you sign the deed of transfer?"

"Yes, here, on the last page. Take a look."

The still, small voice of my conscience was urging me not to look but the shout of my curiosity was more compelling. I turned hurriedly to the final page and there, on the bottom, was the flourished signature, *William Shakespeare*. Another impulse seized me, but this time I didn't bother fighting it. Grabbing Banks by the upper arm, I pulled him to me and hissed, "Mr Banks, you might be purse proud but you are principal poor. In fact, if you had just a little more charm, you'd have all the qualities of a Tyneside dock rat."

Apart from bartering and enjoying such amusements as *Heiva*, or public entertainment similar to a *Punch and Judy* show, the men took part in sports such as swimming, wrestling and archery. Master's Mate Pickersgill was generally regarded as having the best eye, so a competition was organised by Gore to determine who amongst the crew could rightly be crowned champion bowman. Large sums were wagered in favour of Pickersgill, but Master Molyneux and Banks were also considered to have a chance.

It had been another warm day, with an early shower thickening the humidity. As the sun blazed above and droplets hung at the tips of every palm frond on the island, a thousand murmuring spectators gathered around the half-mile perimeter of the arena. Silently, the archers took their positions. Molyneux was the first to compete. His lips were dry and his eyes were an intense blue. As he stood contemplating the task ahead, his thick fingers wriggled themselves into a state of suppleness. Exhaling strongly, he then stepped up to the mark, took aim, and fired. Two seconds later a roar went up from the crowd as the arrow deftly removed a South Sea mango from a tree almost 50 yards away. Molyneux stepped back, smiling with relief and confidence. Pickersgill walked forward. "For someone who couldn't hit the floor if he fell out of bed, you done good. But just you watch this. The money's already in me pocket."

In the cauldron of the arena, the perspiring mate steadied himself by taking two deep breaths. All his concentration was focused on a banana tree 100 yards away. He then drew back the string and fired. Instantly, the spectators let out a howling chorus as Pickersgill peered around.

"Where'd the bloody thing go?" he screamed above the cacophony.

Molyneux stuck his mouth right next to the mate's ear and cupped his hands. "Nowhere," he shouted. "You forgot to put the arrow in, Dead-Eye!"

Banks waited patiently for the deafening derision to stop. There wasn't the slightest hint of fear on his face as he stared defiantly at his rivals. Then, possessed of the arrogant confidence that is typical of all who are born to win, he strode out across the lush grass. The spectators were hushed as Joseph picked up his bow and loaded his arrow. He paused, smiled then looked around at the crowd. They were in the palm of his hand. The bow then came up slowly, his arm drew back and a quick 'ping' signalled the arrow's release. Almost instantly the missile thudded into a stalk of sugar cane 150 yards off. The stalk split in two and to the horror of the spectators, the arrow then re-emerged. Everyone immediately dropped flat to the ground and watched, panic-stricken, as it whistled around the arena, scattered a herd of hogs, knocked over the chief priest's camp fire which in turn set his hut alight then finally embedded itself in a canoe almost 200 yards away.

"I'll be buggered," Banks whispered to me and Gore. "Don't tell anyone, but see that hut over there about ten feet off and to the right? That's what I was aiming at."

All reserve was cast aside in the seconds that followed. Clapping and screaming erupted, as did the flames that quickly spread from the chief priest's hut to the one Joseph had indicated. In an attitude of worshipful respect, the native spectators rushed forward, lifted the botanist high onto their shoulders and carried him away. Three days of feasting followed, and when the hand-fed, milk-bathed idler finally returned to the fort, he was full of himself.

"Men," he said, holding out his soft, white arms in an embarrassingly communal embrace, "they think I'm some sort of demigod, but I wouldn't expect your attitude towards me to change. The occasional boot-buff would be as much as I could ask."

His apparent joke caused us to chuckle, but ten minutes later, when I arrived at my tent, I saw that the joke had gone too far. There, neatly positioned beside the open flap, were Banks' dung-encrusted shoes. The joy I felt from hacking them to pieces with an axe was almost as great as that experienced when I told him what I'd done as we sailed away a short time later. And as the string of islands gradually dissolved into the shimmering blue waters, there wasn't one on board who didn't watch as the ship's broad, foaming wake steadily thinned into a single white line.

It was perhaps the recollection of Otaheite which inspired one of the earliest notes that I drew from the suggestion box. On the 22nd following midday mess, I went below to examine the box's contents. It was a relief to find an easily-opened lid, so I had no trouble in removing the two papers. The first was a demand for two pounds, eight shillings and threepence from 'John Satterley, Esq' for 'Carpentry Services Above & Beyond The Call Of Duty' and the second was a request that appeared to have some merit;

'H.M.S. Endeavour
Sunday 22nd April
1770
Dear Mr Cook,

    I have a complaint about the food Mr Thompson prepares. To put it in terms that one of your class will understand, it's shyte. Those artichokes we took on board in Nieuw Zeeland are wearing very thin. We've had them boiled, stewed, mashed, dried and even raw. If that culinary charlatan offers me another artichoke, I'm going to tell him to stuff it. As you're the man at the helm, might I propose a change of course. If it's forthcoming, you have my word that I'll name a species of insect after you.
Yours sincerely,
J. Banks Esq.'

Leaving aside Banks' attempted belittlement, I had to admit that I shared his feelings. Yet to be fair to John Thompson, or *Gastroguts*, as he was known to the men, he did try hard. Our provisions supplied by the Victualling Board in 1768 had seemed adequate and varied. Among them were 21,000 pounds of bread, 9,000 pounds of flour, 4,000 pieces of beef, 6,000 pieces of pork, 800 pounds of suet, 187 bushels of peas, 2,500 pounds of raisins and 7,860 pounds of sour krout. Added to these were 1,200 gallons of beer, 1,600 of spirits and 500 of vinegar. The vinegar possessed a bitter after-taste, but the more desperate among the ranks found it to their liking. With all of the above, Thompson was able to keep us satisfied for a time following our departure from England. However, before a week had passed, the quality of sameness was becoming worryingly apparent. In an effort to address Banks' complaint regarding the victuals, I made my way to the galley and, as expected, John was hard at it. Not preparing food but hurling pots and pans in all directions. At first he refused to say what had made him so angry but I guessed that it related to the insults that had been thrown his way lately. After some discreet questions, and the mention of Banks' letter, my assumption was confirmed.

"Blimey, Cap'n, I can't do nothin' fancy with artichokes and most of the good stuff had been ate by the time we'd cleared the harbour at the start of the voyage, so if that perfumed grub-bottler writes one more word against me, I'm off."

I quickly pointed out that his choice of destinations was somewhat limited considering we were in the middle of the ocean, but his green eyes narrowed as he replied, "The toffs reckon I should go to blazes or buggery, so there's two places you can stick on the list."

"Take no notice of that lot," I said. "They're like balloons at a fair; bright distractions but light on substance." Then, as a bolster to his flagging confidence, I poured him an extra ration of beer and said encouragingly, "John, you're really doing a fine job under extremely difficult circumstances, but the point is this. The men aren't complaining about the way you present the artichokes. It's just that it's *always* artichokes. Why don't I order the boatswain to organise a fishing party. With fresh fish on their plates, the grizzlers won't have a leg to stand on and we'll both get Banks off our backs."

Thompson agreed, and ten minutes later the boatswain was bellowing out the fishing order to a party of seamen at the stern of the ship. The catch was soon completed and delivered to the galley. An hour passed, and as dusk settled like golden dust upon the sails, the men were piped to their evening meal. As they filed past me, every grimy face beamed with anticipation.

"Enjoy the experience, lads," I said, heading atop, and as soon as I'd reached the poop, a loud 'Hip hip hooray!' echoed through the ship and across the endless ocean. Two minutes later an almighty din erupted below. I dashed through the hatch to the lower deck, only to find the crew, including the officers, holding Thompson upside down and forcing their meals down his throat.

"What's all this bloody fuss about?" I shouted above the riot.

"It's the friggin' fish!" yelled the boatswain as he mashed the contents of his plate into Thompson's thinning, black hair. "Gastro stuffed every one of 'em with stinkin' artichokes!"

As the appointed upholder of law, proper conduct and justice, there was only one thing I could say. However, I chose not to. The men needed to release their frustration, so recalling my mother's advice that a blind eye is sometimes more prudent than an opened mouth, I walked away. As I stooped through the hatch and into the silence of a starry night, the helmsman whispered a greeting; "Pleasant evenin', Captain."

He then nudged the wheel lazily and the ship's massive bulk turned an easy degree to starboard, the timbers and rigging creaking like the joints of an old mariner. High in the sails the wind was humming. All I wanted at that moment was a space and time free of others, so I replied, "For some, Mr Clerke," and paced slowly forward. Reaching the bow, I gazed out across the limitless, rolling tides. Like the wind that pushed against my chest, thoughts of Elizabeth and the children pressed against my heart. A fish leapt from the black water, its silver frozen for an instant in the tarnishing light of a crescent moon. And then it happened; the unexpected that one could count on. A southerly blew up and the images altered. One minute calm, the next confusion. Wind lifting and howling; waves spitting their foam and force against my legs. Cold and concerned about the power that was being unleashed, I wrapped the collar of my coat around my neck and staggered along the greasy deck towards the hatch.

"It's turned nasty mighty quick," Clerke said as he fought the wheel.

I nodded and stepped down into the safety of the companionway. Pausing at Lieutenant Gore's door, I knocked. Things were about to turn a lot nastier. When Gore finally stumbled out of bed and opened up, I said, "Go and tell Banks I want to see him about the letter he put into the box. This food business needs to be cleared up before someone gets killed. I'll be in my cabin."

A little while later, Gore burst into my room. I was drinking a cup of coffee at my desk while I took a break from charting.

"Captain," the lieutenant blurted out, "Mr Banks wasn't there, but I did find this. I think you should take a look!"

He was holding up a piece of paper and, ashen-faced in the glow of the lantern, he placed it on top of the chart. Beads of perspiration glimmered along his top lip. His trembling hands gripped the edge of the desk as the ship lurched. Curious as to the cause of his condition, I glanced down at the page. It contained several paragraphs obviously crafted by Joseph's own careful hand. The words, in the form of hurried scribblings, seared themselves forever into my consciousness: 'The captain is widely despised... despotic... contemptuous of greater intellects... won't listen to reason... frequent headaches... uncontrolled rages... lower class yet aspires to acceptance by his betters... nobody on board respects him and MUTINY seems to be only course of action... can I succeed? Needs careful plotting but I'm confident of outcome... if it fails then I will be criticised... they'll say I shouldn't have tried... I should have stuck to botany. Although I'm afraid, I won't let this fear govern my actions. If only there was someone else on board I could talk to... there isn't... but later someone might be willing to collaborate... check details, times, places events etc... but in this early stage I'll work alone and quietly...'

There it was. As plain as the nose on a spinster's face and twice as sharp. Joseph Banks, a supposed man of honour, was plotting my downfall.

"And see this bit," Gore emphasised as he swept his hand down towards a particular line. In so doing, he knocked the coffee cup and the dark brown liquid spilt and soaked into the paper.

"Now look what you've done!" I shouted as the evidence partially smudged. In trying to minimise his blunder, Gore hurriedly wiped his sleeve across the paper but succeeded only in catching his buttons on the well of my charting ink. What remained of Banks' writing instantly dissolved into the large black blob that spread across the page, the chart underneath and down the side of the desk.

"Now that you've ruined the proof," I said, "there's no way I can confront Banks! As if I didn't have enough on my plate already without this to deal with!"

Gore was trying to make amends by wiping the desk with his coat.

"Leave it alone," I ordered, shoving him towards the door, "or you'll have the lantern over and the ship in flames. Now go back to your cabin and don't breathe a word of this to anyone. All I want you to do is keep a close eye on him and report any unusual behaviour."

"Then you'll be seeing a lot of me because everything he does is loopier than a reef-knot."

That was a prospect almost as dire as the mutiny, and it struck me fairly quickly that Gore's involvement could only make matters worse.

"On second thoughts," I said as I blotted the remaining ink from the desk-top, "forget the last order. Just go back to your cabin and keep your mouth shut. I'll handle Banks in my own way and in my own time."

The remaining days of April dragged themselves across the sand of my being like some groaning, beached turtle. The sun seemed to have given up its life, and when I stared through my porthole at night, the silent shell was as black as suspicion.

Not wanting to succumb to the mood, I set about occupying my time and mind on matters other than Banks' plan. Astronomy was a useful and enjoyable distraction, and so I began an intensive study of the heavens. Unfortunately, Charles Green, the ship's astronomer, heard about it and soon became my second shadow.

Like myself, Charles Green was the son of a Yorkshire farmer, and his dedication to the science of astronomy was well known. It therefore came as no surprise that he was chosen by The Royal Society to be my assistant in the task of observing the Transit of Venus at Otaheite in 1769. Prior to his sailing with me, his professional accomplishments had been considerable, securing him a scientific reputation second-to-none and a place amongst the ranks of gentlemen. His first position of prestige occurred in 1761 when he was appointed to the Greenwich Observatory as assistant to the Astronomer Royal. Then in 1763 he sailed to Barbados with the Reverend Dr Nevil Maskelyne on one of the early evaluations of John Harrison's chronometer. As a lunarite he lacked for nothing, but in the ordinary affairs of men and their associations, Charles was about as useful as a curate in a coal pit. His contempt for sailors as observers was often stated and he adopted a pedant's attitude when called upon to instruct them in his science. Able Seaman Dozey felt the sting of his tongue during one such lesson.

On the 24th, as I stood on the poop marking *Cape St George* bearing West at a distance of almost twenty miles, the able seaman and Charles were within ear-shot on the main deck. It was close to 8 p.m. and the two were discussing the placements of various heavenly bodies.

"You've had a week to learn this," Green had commented, "so can you name the planets in their correct order going out from the sun?"

Even in the shadows, I could see Dozey's brow furrowed in concentration. "I'll try. Mercury, Venus, Earth, Mars, Juniper, Nectarine, Plutarch! How's that?"

"Sweet and Greek but a million miles from science. Here's an easier question." Green then indicated the moon and asked Dozey to explain its position and features. Fairly straight forward, I thought as I continued my watch. Dozey mulled the question over for a minute, rubbed his thumb across the stubble on his chin, pointed heavenward and said confidently, "It's up there, bright and round."

Charles let out a disdainful hiss, grabbed Dozey's head between his large hands, shook it violently and sneered, "Boy, what I'm holding here is a dull object and definitely empty! Find something useless to do below before I dump you overboard."

The shaken sailor glanced at me through the misted, salt-heavy air. He received neither reassurance nor reproof from my blank stare, so he simply picked at some non-existent fluff on his jacket then shuffled into the shadows. When he'd disappeared through the hatch, I called Green to me. A faint, autumn shower was just beginning to dampen the deck as the observer stepped carefully on to the poop.

"Charles," I said, buttoning my coat at the neck, "you were a bit harsh on the lad. He hasn't had the benefits of your sort of education, so try to be a little more patient with him in future."

The drizzle in Green's dark hair ran like silvery rivulets down his cheeks, neck and frilled shirt-front, causing the fabric to cling to his bulging stomach. "How can I be patient with someone who's got the brains of the ship's goat?" he demanded.

"You're doing it again."

"All right, I'll take it back. He doesn't have the brains of the bloody goat. Satisfied?"

I stamped my shoes heavily on the boards, dislodging the surface wetness from my trousers. Then, counting silently to ten, I pinched the material and ran my fingers down to the tops of my sodden shoes. The creases were back. "I may have failed with you," I said tersely, "but at least I've straightened these pants out. And while I can still wear them, even though they're wet, there's no bloody way I can wear you any longer tonight."

As he slipped his way across the deck and lifted the hatch-cover, I shouted above the wet, wolf-howling wind, "**Now** I'm satisfied!"

Not all the causes for the tension amongst the crew were internal to the ship. The natives of the Southern Continent must also take some of the blame. Our first encounter with them occurred during an expedition ashore on the 25th. Accompanying me were Banks, principally so that I could keep a close eye on him, Dr Daniel Solander and Tupia. Dr Solander was the most capable naturalist in England. A Fellow of the Royal Society, Solander had left Sweden in 1759 and in 1763 was appointed to the British Museum on a salary close to sixty pounds a year. Short, stocky and with a thick neck, his appearance was in no way engaging. Nor was his aloof bearing. Gore rightly summed it up as early as Otaheite when he said to me, one day in the fort, that Solander was about as popular as a headache on a honeymoon.

Tupia, a well-born chief *Tahowa*, or priest, of Otaheite, had expressed an interest in experiencing the English way of life, so after a lengthy family discussion, he nervously joined the *Endeavour's* company when we sailed from Matavai Bay on the 13th of July, 1769. Like most of the natives on this island, he was clean, strong and amiable, and I was pleased to have him aboard because he possessed a sound knowledge of the Pacific region and its people.

So when my companions and I landed our yawl on the white, shell-covered shore on the 26th, I was hopeful that Tupia could initiate an understanding between ourselves and the natives. In brotherly fashion, he presented some nails and beads to several loitering in a camp some forty yards off the sand, and they seemed pleased. Their chief, lean and frizzy-haired, remained seated inside his bark hut, both to reinforce his superiority and to shelter from the afternoon humidity, so Tupia approached and started speaking to him. After a few unsuccessful syllables, the islander left the hut, came back to me and said in his Gathrey-tutored English, "No fuggin' luck, Mr Crook. Chief pig-bloody-ignorant."

"At least you tried. And it's Cook."

Dr Solander, intent on making some sort of mark, then stepped forward and offered his hand as a sign of peace. The chief, noticing the gold ring on Solander's right index finger, eagerly gestured for it.

"Captain," the naturalist whispered, taken aback, "I can't possibly hand the ring over to this heathen. It was given to me by my teacher, the great Carl Linnaeus, when I left Sweden."

"Hear me out," I replied, drawing him aside and walking a little way down the beach. "We all cherish things that are of sentimental value but now is not the time to be thinking of yourself in relation to the past. Now is the time to consider the effect you could have on the future. If you give the ring, you could be presenting England with a new land and a grateful ally."

This appeal to Solander's sense of history and duty was, I'd hoped, well-aimed, but the ring remained firmly on his finger. However, a few seconds later he demonstrated a welcome change in attitude when the chief produced his spear and aimed it at what Banks later called the naturalist's more precious 'natural gemstones'.

Having established some sort of tentative bond, we then accepted the chief's invitation to eat with him. Seated in a circle around a central fire, we were offered berries, various winged insects as yet unclassified by even Linnaeus himself and the cooked flesh of lizards. One lizard was particularly plentiful and we'd encountered it almost as soon as we'd stepped foot on shore. It was large, grey and timid, preferring to run quickly away when we approached it. Banks was intrigued by the reptile and he observed that only once before had he witnessed such fleetness of foot. "I don't understand why but one of my estate's more robust chambermaids,

Anna Bolic, runs like the wind whenever she sees me," he said as the reptile disappeared into the scrub behind the beach, "and because of the creature's remarkable agility, I declare that it will henceforth be called 'Lacerta Celeri' or 'Swift Lizard'."

Here was an opportunity to have some sport with the brabbling irritant and I seized it. "Joseph, your eminent position demands a far less prosaic nomenclature, so why not reference it to yourself. Keep the running part and add the most deserving name."

"Good idea," the beaming botanist said. "You mean something like 'RunawayBanks Lizard'?"

"No. Your chambermaid's unsurprising alacrity is central to the process so its official name is now 'Goanna'."

Banks was still smarting as we sat with our native hosts, and even though the food was foreign to our European palates, we tried as best we could to enjoy it.

"How are your lizards, Dr Solander?" I asked as Daniel popped one into his mouth.

"Well, the Blue-Tongue could do with some spice, perhaps a little coriander, but this Frill Neck is delicious. I wonder if there's any more. I say, Tupia, can I have another frill?"

Tupia smiled generously and wiggled the chief's eating stick up Daniel's trouser leg.

"I don't think that's quite what the doctor had in mind," Banks suggested patronizingly.

Concerned about his reluctance to fully join in the festivities, I leaned over and told him to tuck in. He ignored my order and made his attitude even more obvious by repeatedly dry-retching like a cat with a fur ball when the chief offered him a species of white grub. Fearful that his action might be viewed by our hosts as provocative, I grabbed the grub and stuffed it into my own mouth. Even though the wretched thing tasted vile, I chewed it quickly and swallowed. Almost at once it was clear that the chief still felt slighted because he let out some sort of primitive, growling noise, picked up one of the campfire rocks and hurled it towards Banks. Acting instinctively, I immediately fired a musket load of small shot above the aggressors' heads. The campsite cleared almost as quickly as the smoke, and the nearby woods echoed with the screams of fleeing, terrified heathens. Under the cover of the closing darkness, we then made our way back to the yawl. As we rowed towards the *Endeavour* through a choppy, blue-black sea, Solander, puffing heavily between strokes, said, "So much for the new land and grateful ally you said I'd be presenting to England. I had a ring that no amount of money could buy, and now I've lost it."

"You've still got your renowned capacity for excruciating self-pity," Banks sneered as he pretended to row, "so shove a cork in it and keep paddling."

"You can both shove a cork in it!" I spat into the chilling air. From that moment on, the only noise heard was the regular slap of oar on water. On board the ship twenty minutes later and relieved at finding themselves within the safe confines of my suite, Solander and Banks wasted no time, and displayed no reserve, in criticising one another. The thick, green baize that covered the floor went some way to absorbing the fury, but the clamour was nonetheless deafening. Solander, with the veins in his neck protruding, accused his colleague of endangering our lives by refusing to eat the grub.

Banks grabbed the brass scale from the plane table near the door and menacingly waved it in Solander's direction. "Then why didn't *you* eat it?" he demanded.

"Because I was leaving room for the smoked snake!"

"Smoked snake!" Banks shouted. "Nobody offered *me* smoked snake! Were you offered the snake, Captain?"

"Yes," I said with some hesitation, not wishing to inflame the situation further, "but I was more than happy just to pick at the hornets."

Banks banged the scale back onto the table, adjusted his red silk waistcoat, and complained, "Bloody typical! There we were, picnicking with the primitives and surrounded by inedible muck. Suddenly some snake appeared, probably more than you could shake a stick at, and was I told? No!"

As he stormed from my cabin, he turned, pointed a threatening finger at Solander and said, "If I wasn't such a gentleman, I'd invite you onto the deck and have Briscoe kick the shit out of you." The door then slammed shut.

In the mahogany bookcase attached to the starboard wall, the library of navigation and natural history references shook violently, causing several to tumble onto the baize. As Solander stooped to retrieve them, he knocked over the lantern that was keeping the charts flattened on my desk. Splinters of glass showered the smoothly varnished top and came to rest along the parallel ruler and in the space between the dividers. The unmistakeable smell of smouldering wool quickly filled the quarters, so I shoved him aside and stamped my boot down heavily. Fortunately, the damage was minimal. Solander slumped into my chair and sighed with relief. "You put that out quickly."

"And you're going out just as fast," I said, dragging him up, opening the door and pushing his fat frame vigorously. To get rid of the stench, I then opened the porthole and sniffed deeply. A faint eucalyptus freshness drifted in, carried from the land by a steady westerly.

I bent slowly, untied my shoe laces and flopped onto my bunk. And then it struck, like a hammer blow to the head; I'd been so pre-occupied with settling this latest squabble that I'd forgotten about the treachery Banks was planning. The thought thumped at my temples. He hadn't yet made any obvious move so there was nothing I could do except wait. It was this waiting, coupled with the concerns I felt about my own safety, which brought on an even stronger pain; home-sickness.

Nothing could replace the feeling of comfort I'd experienced in my cottage back here in Mile End. Not even the relative snugness of the Great Cabin in my ship. The *Endeavour* had originally been a coal carrier called the *Earl of Pembroke*, and had been refitted at His Majesty's Dockyard at Deptford in the early months of 1768. According to the commissioning committee of surveyors and master shipwrights, she was ideally suited for voyages of discovery, being a bark large enough for provisions, cannon and boats and yet small enough to be beached and repaired, should the need have arisen. She also had a shallow draft which enabled safe sailing near to land. However, internal space was a constant problem. The civilians and officers were berthed aft under the poop with some degree of satisfaction, but the crew, more than 80, was a tangle of arms, legs and swinging hammocks competing for an individual patch of space above the stores on the lower deck. Any meagre nook that wasn't occupied by a sailor housed either the cookroom items, the carpenters' essentials or the boatswain's stores. All this and more squeezed inside a vessel just on 100 feet in length. It was like trying to stuff a giraffe into a snuff-box.

Yet for all her damp discomfort, the ship was, in most respects, dependably sound, and my suite had been something of a small haven. However, autumn winds, cold waters and failing friendships brought with them the change in my mood. Whenever I lay my head down, thoughts of Elizabeth, our children and my cottage troubled me so much that I found it almost impossible to sleep. Not that my dwelling in the hamlet of Mile End Old Town could in any way be regarded as extravagant. In fact, quite the reverse. Indeed, as I'm writing, I can even now hear the drunken revelling in the nearby Assembly Rooms, and the noxious fumes of the adjacent distillery are churning my stomach. Yet it's my home; a safe harbour. Elizabeth brings me tea when I need refreshment and the chattering Boswell calls in and gossips when I'm desperate for diversion. At night I sleep in a bed that doesn't rise, rock or roll, and during the day I can please myself regarding the company I keep.

However, the treasured moments are kept for that hour following supper each evening. After the plates have been cleared, I go into the sitting-room and wait for my sons, Nathaniel and James. Before long there is a soft knock on the door. It opens and there they stand, white-haired and smiling. When I nod, they charge into my arms and beg for tales of far-away places. As I speak, it doesn't take long for the lilt of my voice to carry them away. I then carry them to bed. It was for a return to these boys and their mother that I craved so often during the latter part of the voyage. And I also longed to be with my other children, Joseph and Elizabeth.

Joseph had been born only days following my departure, so I was never able to be a cradle for his frailty or tickle his rolling chin or watch his eyes move slowly around the new mystery of it all. In my heart I had hoped for his baptism before the ship left, but this wasn't to be, so I had none of these moments to take with me as a blanket against the chill of missing.

Elizabeth, my only daughter, with hair and skin as pale as whispering, was twelve months old when I sailed. It had been a special year; a time of softening. I worried over the slightest sniffle, wondered what her thoughts were when she looked at me, encouraged when she tried to crawl and laughed when she couldn't. Every morning I thanked God for her being and her continuing. During long nights away, when the sky was clear, the sea calm and the wind a hush through my hair, I used to recall how her tiny hand had gripped my finger. She would then reach up, pat my eyes and smile. The image of her smile lifted me during my three-year absence and I remember the excitement I felt at the thought of seeing her again when we finally anchored in the Downs at the end of the voyage. If only I'd sailed a short time later and come home a little earlier. Joseph died a month after I'd departed. Elizabeth died three months before I returned. There is no more to be said on these matters. We are all now at home in our harbours.

Another type of harbour, or rather, bay, was occupying my attention the day following our excursion ashore. We'd sailed close to it during the night, and it appeared that the area would permit an extended stay. It was the morning of the 26th. The weather was clear, with variable light airs between north-east and north-west. We stood off shore until 10 o'clock, then tacked. Mr Hicks ordered a sounding, so the pinnace put out. The lead and line indicated the water's depth to be more than 30 fathoms. No hindrance to safe navigation. Land was some two miles off, and because we were beating against a headwind, I called for another tack so as to manoeuvre closer in. At once the headsheets were eased off, the spanker hauled to wind'ard, the fore tack and sheet let go and the mainsail hauled up. As the ship swung across the wind, all the main and mizzen yards were hauled round, while the backed head-yards with their sails pressed the ship's head further until the main and mizzen yards were behind the wind. Finally, with the wind flowing into those sails, the foreyards were hauled round and the *Endeavour* gathered headway. For once I was pleased with the men's efforts because they had shown what sailors should be; competent and co-operative. Seizing the all-too-rare opportunity for praise, I issued a loud and general 'Well done'.

Near to 11, we found ourselves a mile closer to land, and from this distance I could see the gradual change in the colour of the water. Under us, it was deep blue. Nearer the shore, it was a lighter blue, indicating a sandy bottom. The patches of green showed the presence of weed. The weed, in turn, suggested the probability of fish. Waves, with small heads of foam, followed one another onto the beach, their energies being swallowed by the sand. Standing back from the beach, like a regiment of the King's finest, was a profusion of pines and palms. Some of the palms were as high as sixty feet, and they were similar in many respects to those we had sighted in Otaheite a year earlier. Their tops swayed, pushed to and fro by the gentle insistence of a sou'easterly. In between the trees and spaced at regular intervals were clusters of small, brown shelters. I assumed that these were the natives', so I called Tupia to my side on the poop and asked him about them.

"They called friggin' *buckets*," he replied.

"Buckets! That's absurd. Buckets are things water comes in."

The boatswain, who'd been doing nothing in particular near the wheel, sauntered over. "Cap'n," he said, "as you know, I've been learnin' old Tup how to speak effluent English, so let me explain. He didn't say friggin' buckets. He said friggin' bark huts. And while we're gabbin' on about speakin' good, you just said water comes in buckets. It don't. It comes in friggin' holes in the hatches. Absolutely pisses in."

My cold stare in response was more effective than a hot-tempered dressing down. Gathrey grabbed Tupia's arm and the two quickly walked away. Silence then settled on the sails and rigging. With just a hint of a wind brushing across my forehead, I gazed at the land. God had given to it a rare fruitfulness. Even the air was fecund, teeming with sea birds that squawked above the masts then flapped away into faint white specks long before they reached the horizon.

It was the sort of moment that needed to be shared, so when I saw the back of a head emerge through the main hatch, I raised my hand and beckoned. When Banks stepped out, my arm dropped. There was no way I could welcome such a two-faced hypocrite, so I turned my back. As I did, it occurred to me that if I showed some sort of interest towards him, perhaps even kindness, then the ship's calculated destruction might at best be set aside or at worst delayed long enough for me to catch him out. Not only for my safety, but also the men's. With a faint smile, I turned around and said, "Come stand beside me and see what the Lord has made. We should rejoice and be glad in it."

"Indeed we should," Joseph agreed as he joined me on the poop. With his spirit soaring, he opened his mouth widely and sang, "Oh for a thoooooousand tongues to sing, my great Redeemer's praise, my greeeeeat Redeemer's praaaaise."

The jarring flatness of the hymn's rendition made me grateful to the Redeemer that He had supplied Banks with 999 fewer than the number requested. Having sung himself almost hoarse, Joseph then reached for the pad and sketching equipment that he had brought from his cabin. When they were neatly arranged within easy reach, he propped himself against the starboard rail and started drawing the shore-line with its wide expanse of sand and trees just beyond.

"That's not too bad," I said, feigning interest as I looked over his shoulder, "but why have you placed the trees in the water?"

"Trees need water, so ipso facto, trees and water go together."

"True," I said, coming down off my tip-toes, "but not those trees and not that water."

Banks churlishly erased the trees and repositioned them.

"That's better," I encouraged, "but they're not actually growing on the beach. If you look through the 'scope you'll see they're further back on the grassed area."

Banks raised the 'scope to his eye. "All right, you've made your point! Is there anything else you want to criticise?"

"Joseph," I said, trying to placate him, "I was suggesting, not criticising. And as you've asked, there are a couple of things. The native girl. I see you've drawn her in profile but there are two eyes showing instead of one. And she seems rather flat, almost geometric."

Banks placed the pad on the deck then sharpened his pencil with a small knife. The sun reflecting off the blade made me blink as he said, "For your information, I'm experimenting with a new form of expression. It's an attempt to find a type of internal truth that isn't obviously related to external appearance. It's a radical departure from sentimentality and emotionalism."

"That's interesting. It certainly seems well ahead of its time. Do you have a name for this new style?"

The botanist's answer was immediate. "Squarism."

"Squarism? That doesn't sound too bad but I must be honest. I don't think it'll ever amount to much as a movement."

"Why not?" Banks asked huffily. "Significant changes only occur when one man has a singular vision and a limitless capacity to endure."

"That's the problem. By definition, men of singular vision are one-eyed and therefore limited."

Banks plunged his knife into the deck. "Very pithy," he said as he stared at the trembling handle. "Now what was the other thing you wanted to mention?"

Conscious of my inferior social standing, I was reluctant to continue. However, to gain some degree of equal footing, I did. "It's only a minor point but it's valid. Those trees that fill the page. Are they palms?"

Banks raised his eyebrows contemptuously and said, "Of course. Do poplars have coconuts?"

"Now I understand. Squarism equals square coconuts. I'm almost afraid to ask this, Joseph, but here goes. If they're palm trees, why are they pink instead of green?"

"Not *all* palms are green!" the botanist scoffed. "Here, I'll prove it. Tip us your daddle and tell me what you see."

"I will not! My doodle, to use your coarse term, is for my wife's eyes only!"

"I didn't say doodle. It was daddle... your hand... show me your hand... good... so what do you see?"

Unsure as to the destination of Banks' train of thought, I said tentatively, "Knuckles, thick veins, some hair."

"Turn it over."

The end of the line suddenly came into view and a sense of defeat welled up within me.

"What do you see now?"

I bit my lip as I replied, "My palm."

"And what colour is it?"

At that moment, two or three yards off the port bow, a huge, silver-grey stingray glided just under the surface of the water. I deliberately kept my eyes fixed on its languid movement.

"Come on, Mr Cook, you have to answer some time."

"It's pink."

"Pardon? I couldn't hear properly."

"I said my palm is pink! You may have scored a point just now but let me remind you that we play under my rules. Don't ever try to take advantage of our relationship again. You may not be one of the ratings, but if you attempt to humiliate me in future, or try anything else that might be seen as a direct threat to my authority, I'll treat you in exactly the same fashion as any other insubordinate."

Having reaffirmed my position, and hinted that his planned subversion was not the secret he'd imagined, I left him to his doodling and sought the 2nd lieutenant. I found him checking the soundness of the backstays supporting the top-masts. Because I was still smarting from my recent belittlement, I yelled at him to forget what he was doing and organise a fishing party in order to supply the cook with fresh victuals. Within twenty minutes, a dozen able seamen assembled on deck and cast their lines over the lee rail. For once they seemed content, most chatting or humming as they pulled in a swag of colourful fish. After an hour's work the deck was strewn with more than 80, the odd one still flipping and flopping around the sun-stiffened remainder. By this time Banks had finished his sketching, so he joined Lieutenant Hicks and me as we inspected the catch.

The botanist's curiosity regarding a completely black specimen was aroused, so he said to Hicks as he nudged it with his shoe, "What is this known as?"

Now Hicks was a man not easily tempted into sarcasm, but this was an opportunity too good to miss. "I'm surprised you don't recognise it," he said, glancing slyly in my direction. "If I'm not mistaken, it's called your boot."

"Highly risible," Banks said dryly as he grabbed Hicks' shoulders and spun him around, "and if *I'm* not mistaken, that's your arse so allow me to introduce the former to the latter."

"Stick it up your own," the lieutenant yelled as he broke free and scurried away.

Several minutes later, the botanist, by now exhausted from watching all the work that had gone on around him, went below to his cabin for a sleep. There was a chuckle in my throat as I helped the men gather in their lines. When we'd finished, I noticed that the weed that had clung to them had stained my hands. Within a minute I was standing beside Banks' bed. With a couple of hefty thrusts, I shook the sleeper awake, shoved my hands into his face and said, "Take a good, long look and tell me what you see."

Banks rubbed his eyes, squinted in the dimness, and said, "I don't know; your hands, palms. Let me go back to sleep."

"Later. Now tell me what colour they are."

He rolled over, his face towards the cabin wall. I quickly rolled him back.

"Come on, Banks, the colour?"

"Green," he said, his voice muffled by his pillow.

"I can't hear you. Take that thing off your mouth."

"I said your palms are green!" he shouted, covering his frown of humiliation with a blanket. Peeking under the covers, I said, with just the slightest tone of self-satisfaction, "Never play the game with the one who sets the rules. Now sleep tight and when you wake we'll take a stroll up on the quarter-deck and continue our discussion about art. You have a rare gift." I was tempted to add, "It's a pity it's not extinct" but decided that his wounded pride would heal faster without the addition of a salty remark.

As I was checking the workings of the windlass an hour later, Joseph staggered over to me, his unsteadiness the result of the side-to-side rolling as the ship cut through the water. His ludicrous headwear indicated that he was sympathetic to my earlier suggestion regarding an art discussion.

"Nice beret, Mr Banks."

"Thanks. If it was good enough for Rembrandt, it's good enough for me. After all, what did he have that I haven't?"

I chewed my lip pensively for a moment and replied, "An eye for detail, a capacity for draughting, an understanding of colour, an appreciation of form, a flair for design and balance, a knowledge of perspective, an aesthetic spirit, a reasoned philosophy regarding all things visible and invisible..."

Adjusting the beret so that it was on a slight tilt, Banks interrupted, "There you go again, nit-picking. You really are an insufferable pedant."

The afternoon heat was intense and there was no relieving breeze from the water. An albatross circled around the ship, imaging the one that was around my neck. I stared at Banks, uncertain as to what to say next. He stared back at me, unsure of why I was staring at him. A slight smile creased the corners of my mouth. A concerned frown crinkled the skin of Joseph's brow. My smile grew into a large grin and then I laughed. The more I stared the louder I laughed, and the louder I laughed, the more worried Joseph became.

"You're carrying on like a lunatic, Mr Cook. Have you gone mad?"

"No, but you will be. I'm laughing because the albatross has just scrawled its rather sticky signature on the top of that putrid cat mat on your head."

Just at that moment I noticed Dr Solander lurking behind the fore-mast at the bow of the ship, savouring his colleague's embarrassment and intent upon further eavesdropping. Remembering my intention to show Banks some degree of kindness, for a purpose more imperative than friendship, I apologised for finding humour in his misfortune and suggested we bury the hatchet. Before he could respond, Solander sauntered by and sniggered, "And at the same time you should hatchet that shitty beret."

The following morning during breakfast, I recounted this incident to the officers and we all laughed till our ribs almost cracked. I may not have won Banks over, but the memory of him standing there with his bare face hanging out beneath a beretful of bird-shit often lightened my concern during the weeks that followed.

When breakfast and laughter finished at roughly the same time, I went back to my cabin to check the suggestion box. There was only one piece of paper inside. It read:

'KapTin.,
i fiNk it wOOde BE a good ider if yOO got to No yor mEN more beTter.?. hoW aBout haveing CHats with toO or three of US at A tyme..! we cooD drINk tee and eaT sum littLe cayks and we coOD tork aboUt our hoBbeys?. lyke in mY kase itS breedin pet moUSes and helpin GastroGUts in the GAlleE;? i MESelf perSONL like REkon if yOO spend sum tYme with us inforMal like yoo mite be able to understAnd us proper;:? becorse we Are human Beans, onest wee IS,, iF yoo giT toO like us yoo mite Stop yeLLin at us eVRy day.!; ANd maybeE yoo mite not Git so meny bad Hedakes and yOo mite stoP lockin Yorself in Yor kabbin so that yoo Dont see our orrible Little faeces like wHat yoo Allways say;,!?.
MErry CriSMis kAptin? fRom yor freND!
(!PS ON - i Git a woBBly Tummy if i eat a cayk wHat has ChokLit in it?? – P!S OFF!))'

The writer's words, although penned by someone several planks shy of a complete hull, made me think that perhaps I'd been so busy carrying out the commission given to me by the Admiralty that I'd overlooked the nurturing of personal relationships; that my inadvertent neglect was, in fact, partly responsible for their deterioration. I wasn't willing to concede the point, but for the sake of future harmony, I decided to follow up on the suggestion.

The first step was to consult the muster roll. Having done so, I then ordered the boatswain to have two nominated crewmen meet me on the quarter-deck in ten minutes. His other task was to have the cook send up some tea and oat cakes.

At the appointed time I went atop and eyed the two men chosen. They were standing on either side of the wheel, trousers stained and creased, shirt buttons pushed through the wrong holes and cheeks shadowed with grime and stubble. When they saw me, they quickly tried to slick down their hair with one or two shots of spit. The feeling I got was that here were two wayward schoolboys expecting to be thrashed by the headmaster, so to put their minds at ease, I said, "It's good to see you, Midshipman Saunders, and you also, Able Seaman Matthews. Please, sit down."

Saunders stared with stunned amazement. He was participating in a naval revolution and his head was obviously spinning.

I pointed to the refreshments and said, "Tea, gentlemen?"

Saunders nodded. "Don't mind if I do. Shall I play 'mother'?"

"Just pour."

"Right. Say *when* Sir."

A minute passed without the slightest movement from Saunders so I asked him why he hadn't poured the tea.

"I asked you to tell me when, remember?"

"**Now**, you fuc... sorry... pour now, thanks Mr Saunders."

The midshipman flapped his hands nervously, and as he picked up the pot and poured, I handed the oat cakes to Matthews. He reached out tentatively, withdrew his hand then said, "They ain't got no choklit in 'em, 'ave they?"

What a stroke of good fortune. "So it was **you** who thought up this scheme? Tell me about your family."

Matthews squinted as the glare reflecting off the water met his gaze. "Well, Sir, I'm the oldest of sixteen kids. Me old man's dead, no bleedin' wonder, and me mum takes in washin', always at night and from rich people's hangin' lines."

"And do you have any brothers in the armed services?"

Matthews shovelled in another oat cake and spluttered, "No, but me uncle served time for armed robbery a few years back. Does that make 'im a sailor or soldier?"

I took a sip of my tea, hoping that the warm sweetness might go some way towards lessening the bitter tension that was just starting to throb at my temples. "No, it makes him a thug and a thief."

"But, Skipper, all of us on this tub is thugs and thiefs but the navy signed *us* up."

This time I took a huge gulp of the tea. "I've heard enough, thank you, Matthews. Mr Saunders, let's hear something interesting from you."

Saunders crossed his legs, "Like what?"

"Your parents. Are they still living?"

"Yes, they've got a small cottage in Kent. In fact, me mother, bless her heart, made a bit of a name for herself a few years back. She was disgusted with the way the area was becoming spoiled with all sorts of rubbish. None of the bigwigs gave a hoot about tidying the place up so mum, being fairly strong-minded, organised a band of washer women to do the job. The group was called 'Mothers Unite to Clean Kent' or 'MUCK' for short."

"It's just as well she didn't organise a *fathers'* group," Matthews chortled with crumbs cascading down his shirt-front. He then poured himself another cup of tea and asked, "Listen, doesn't anyone want to 'ear about me 'obbies? I brought one up t' show youse."

"What is it?" Saunders said, moving to the edge of his chair.

From his shirt pocket, and with immense pride, Thomas produced a dirty great grey rat with twenty-inch whiskers and teeth the size of Moses' tablets.

"How adorable," Saunders twittered. "A field-mouse. Have you given it a name?"

"Too right. It's 'Jimmy', just like what the skipper's is."

"Well, I never," Saunders gushed. "You named him after the captain. That's beautiful. He's certainly got the captain's eyes. Where'd you find him?"

"Nowhere. I bred 'im, down in the 'old. And there's another forty."

Saunders was tapping his toes excitedly. "A *family*! Captain, did you hear that? We've got a family on board!"

As I was about to launch my boot into the rodent's rear, it leapt from Matthews' grimy hand and clamped its teeth firmly onto the midshipman's nose.

"Look, Captain," Saunders said, "he's playing with me. What a friendly little Jimmy you are. Oh, he's playing a bit harder now. Thomas, could you ask him not to bite so hard?... Thomas, he's really digging in. Would you please take him away! Ouch! Look, I'm bleeding! YOOWWWW! Call the friggin' doctor!... someone get a musket! Matthews, don't just sit there, get this vicious great bastard off me! EEOOOOOWWWWW!"

The sight of Saunders rolling around the deck with the rat hanging off the end of his swollen conk caused me to convulse with stifled laughter. Breathing deeply to compose myself, I then told Matthews to get it off Saunders or else I was going to shove it into a cannon and blow it twenty miles out to sea. Huffily, Matthews plucked the gnashing rodent from Saunders' nose and said with affection, "Who's been a naughty Jimmy, then? I'll give you one last tickle and it's back into me pocket. We can't 'ave you showin' off like that. Me friends will fink I 'aven't learnt you proper manners."

Saunders, by now returning to some sort of coherency, got up off the deck and steadied himself on the poop's rail. "Matthews," he snarled, feeling his nose gingerly, "everyone reckons you're a complete nick ninny but I know you're not because nobody's perfect."

The able seaman's face turned bright red as he jumped up and shouted, "Was that an insult, Cap'n?"

There was no point in trying to retrieve the situation, so I stood to attention, even though the ship was listing, and replied, "Shut up. Trying to do anything positive around here is like trying to piss into a thimble during a hurricane. So you can both fuck off and Matthews, the minute you get below, get rid of those disease-drenched vermin. If I see so much as a whisker when I inspect the hold later, you'll both be hauled up before the Admiralty when we return to England."

Sufficiently chastised, the two marched off. As I stood on the poop surveying the tree-spiked hills to port, a sudden, strong wind came up, billowing the main topsail.

"Maintain a steady course north," I told the helmsman as I passed the wheel. I may not have been getting very far with the men, but at least the ship was moving forward.

That was the only thought that kept my spirit buoyant when the incident involving Able Seaman James Magra arose sometime close to the 28th of April. Having to deal with it meant that I couldn't fully concentrate on the more dire matter of Banks' plot, and it also caused the men to be even more suspicious of one another.

The *Endeavour* was anchored a few hundred yards from shore, in the Latitude 34°10'South. A gentle nor'easterly was caressing the ship, drying the deck and rigging which had been drenched by a heavy downpour during the night. Lieutenant Hicks and I had just finished inspecting the magazine and were preparing to put out in the pinnace in order to sound the surrounding waters when Master's Mate Charles Clerke approached us. The droop in his mouth told me that he was about to batter my ears with another complaint. A familiar conversation in a foreign country.

The gist of his gripe was that at an hour well past midnight, while he'd been "sleeping deep in the arms of Morpheus", someone had stolen his timepiece. Hicks tut-tutted, shook his head and said something about going below to check the muster rolls. A few minutes later he rejoined me atop, armed with what he thought was vital information.

"Captain, we must have a stowaway on board because there's no 'Seaman Morpheus' listed on the rolls. And I've looked everywhere but he's definitely gone. So it's my guess that the swine must have done a bunk after he'd pinched Clerke's timepiece."

"You're a boring defective."

"Pardon?"

"I said you're a born detective."

During this conversation, I'd noticed that Clerke, tall as a tale from a Dublin drunkard and thin as a politician's promise, had been impatiently shifting from one foot to the other, and while Hicks mulled the whole thing over, the master's mate insisted that the matter be taken further as he believed that the thief was still on board. As did I.

With my temper aroused because of yet another complaint that forced me to abandon essential seamanship, I ordered the pinnace to be relashed and told the boatswain to assemble the crew. When the men were finally lined up, I strode to the poop under a coal-smeared sky and stood to attention. There didn't seem any point in embroidering the crime by stressing the need for trust or appealing to a guilty conscience, so I simply mentioned the theft and demanded the culprit own up.

The sun beat with an almost audible pulse in the silence down the ranks. No-one moved. I watched and waited, and the seconds ticked heavily on. Eventually one of the men cracked his knuckles as a relief to the tension. This prompted others to shift slightly and before long there was general agitation as throats were cleared and dew beaters shuffled. One or two perspiring heads then turned towards the centre of the deck, and soon every eye was fixed accusingly on the figure leaning on the mainmast, Able Seaman James Magra.

"What are youse all starin' at me f'r?" he said.

I wasn't surprised to see Magra accused in this way. Often drunk and belligerent, he was a rogue of the lowest order. Before the voyage, his life in London was blotted by shady incidents and seamy companions. He stole, went with harlots, lied to all and sundry, gambled on everything, fought in taverns and regularly associated with actors. There wasn't a magistrate in the city who hadn't dealt with him, but always on a strict, cash-only basis, according to the boatswain. Rumours and innuendo aside, there was one fact no-one could dispute; James 'The Maggot' Magra was a good-for-nothing.

I looked the midshipman directly in the eye and coldly told him that I wanted the truth. Then, at the height of the tension I'd successfully created, Banks pushed his way through the ranks, whippet in tow, and said, "Truth's an interesting concept, Mr Cook. There are many types; theological, scientific, metaphysical, philosophical. I think it would help Magra if you were a bit more specific."

"Banks," I said, moving towards him. "You want specific truth? Here it is. I'm going to kick the shit out of you."

"You're on your own, Magra," Banks said, stepping back hurriedly.

Totally abandoned, the midshipman affected a look of innocent outrage and replied, "T'weren't me what stole it, Cap'n."

This look of innocence continued even as the small clock which he'd concealed in the back of his trousers started chiming 11 a.m.. As the final 'ding' echoed around the brine-bleached deck, he shot a quick glance over his shoulder and exclaimed, "Bugger me dead! How'd that get there? Straight up, someone's just lumbered me with this!"

Hicks then took over the inquiry, but none of his questions resulted in anything that a court would construe as a confession. I sensed that Magra, skilled at lying through his yellow teeth, was slowly sailing away on the fair winds of Hicks' unskilled probing, so it was time for a more direct tack.

"Magra," I said in a deliberately cold tone, "how would you like to scrape the barnacles from the ship's hull while we're travelling at a rate of knots under full sail?"

"I was only lendin' it off him for a while," Maggot quickly coughed up.

"You disgust me," I said. "Where are your scruples?"

"Down here," the Maggot replied, pointing to the front of his breeches, "where they've always been."

His chances of receiving even the slightest show of leniency immediately vanished, and following my finding of guilt, he was then paraded on deck under a crackling sun, stripped to the waist, bound to an upturned grating and flogged while Drummer Rossiter beat time to the six strokes. I then relieved him of any duty within the ship for seven days.

Later that afternoon, as Hicks and I were discussing the theft in the coolness of the Great Cabin, the lieutenant asked if I'd been serious about keel-hauling Magra under full sail. Zachariah's eyes, blue and quizzical, half-closed as he awaited my reply, and his anticipation hung in the hollow like an uncertain hummingbird. I sat forward in my chair, took a sip of coffee and said, "What do you reckon?"

"I think you would have shown the wretch compassion."

I added a dash more sugar, stirred and, as if in a confessional, drew myself close to Zachariah. "You're right. I would've reduced sail."

Again Hicks lathered his language with the soft soap of sycophancy. "You're a true commander. If anyone deserves to be the First Lord of the Admiralty, it's James Cook. How on earth John Montagu got the job is beyond me. I tell you, if there is a war with our American colonies, as seems inevitable, then England is in serious trouble. With Lord Sandwich in charge of our naval forces, I doubt that we could beat an egg with a wooden spoon."

"We couldn't even *find* an egg," I said, opening the door. "The conceited old fool uses every one laid as filling for those silly bread things he invented. Now I've just remembered something I've got to finish here so I want you and Gore to take the pinnace out."

It was the end of the month and therefore time to award the prize for the best suggestion, so I stepped outside to remove any last-minute deposits in the box. The diversion was welcome because it briefly took my mind off Banks. Although the pretender hadn't yet shown his callous-free hand, my bones told me he would. The box contained very little of interest. If I recall correctly, there was only a death threat against the entire crew signed by Gastro and a chain letter from Matthews stating that if it wasn't passed on, 'EvrY offisers Bigg FAT ArSe will berst iNto FLamEs the NEXt tyme theres a fuLL MOONE!,;?.'

When I'd decided upon the winning suggestion, not because it was the best but because it was the least offensive, I ordered the boatswain to assemble the crew on the main deck for the prize-giving ceremony. "And ask Mr Gore to come to me immediately. I feel a fever coming on so I want him to conduct the ceremony."

Shortly after, as I discussed my choice and the reasons for it with the 3rd lieutenant on the poop, a rush of activity went on around us. Feet scurried up through hatches and arms hauled as the anchor was weighed and the main-sail lowered.

"Furl it!" was the general order.

"Fuck it!" was the usual response.

When the ship finally settled upon a slate-smooth sea, a sense of anticipation rippled through the ranks. This was a formal ceremony, so the 3rd lieutenant began the proceedings with what he considered to be an appropriate speech.

"Friends, Romans, sailormen. Lend me your ears."

A moment of frantic unbuttoning followed before Gore's shrill voice sought to rectify the general misunderstanding. "Stop it! The word was 'ears', so will you all please pull up your breeches and turn back this way."

When every exposed rear was upright and mercifully out of sight, Gore continued. "Men, the captain has gathered you here this afternoon to award the monthly prize to the fellow who made the best suggestion for improving morale. But first, let me explain how the decision was reached."

"How's about just tellin' us who won what?" shouted a familiar voice from the centre of the ranks. Several of the crew started cat-calling and whistling at Peckover, while one or two others standing beside the long-boat let out blurting noises. This blathering on deck was imaged by the tizz of terns that perched high and noisily along the foresail yard, and my enthusiasm for this occasion was rapidly waning. Impatience and fever were taking their toll but as captain I had to endure. Wanting to end the proceedings as quickly as possible, I shoved Gore to one side and stepped to the front of the poop.

"Men," I said, steadying myself on the rail, "this month's winner is the person who suggested the practice of holding regular and informal chats."

With an unexpected surge, my fever worsened, causing my knees to buckle. Reluctantly, I asked Gore to again take over.

"Aye aye. Now, first prize... hang on. Stand easy." He then turned to me and said quietly, "What is it?"

From the corner of my mouth I whispered that it was a bottle of port.

Gore copied my action. "***That's*** first prize? Shit, they'll have us scragged from the yardarm! What's second?"

"I don't know. I'm too ill to care. Ask Hicks."

The 3rd lieutenant turned to Hicks, who was standing behind me, and raised his eyebrows.

"Two of the same," Hicks said.

Gore swallowed and shifted uneasily. "Men," he said, weighing each word, "I'm going to keep it a surprise, but I can tell you it's an absolute bottler. Would the person responsible for making the suggestion please fall out and be recognised."

As soon as he'd finished the sentence, the entire crew fell out and fell over each other in the rush. Summoning what remained of my flagging strength I drew myself to attention and shouted, "Get back into ranks! For the next two weeks it's only a half ration of rum per day. And if there's any more of this unruliness, you'll be confined aboard ship for a month."

The men's silence indicated their compliance. As I continued to stare them down, my legs got the shakes. Hicks noticed my febrile unsteadiness, grabbed my arms and shouted for the surgeon. Delirium overwhelmed me and I dropped. It was all too much. The pains. The questions. The answers. Never-ending. One after the other. War-drums in my head and words in my ears; *BOOM! BOOM! Cap'n, Sir! Someone stole this, someone said that. Who did it? He did it. Hey diddle diddle, the ship's cat's done a piddle. It's raining, it's pouring, the captain is snoring.*

"Shhh... don't wake him. He needs all the sleep he can get."

The voices had the opposite effect and my eyes wearily opened. Gore's face slowly came into focus. Hicks was standing next to him, looking down with concern.

"What time is it?" I whispered. "Where am I and what happened?"

"It's midnight," Hicks said, "and we're in your cabin. You passed out at the ceremony earlier. Is there anything you want?"

My eyes closed involuntarily. "The pleasure of your absence. Good night."

Eerie shadows from the flickering lamp moved across the ceiling, their cotillion in sympathy with the music and rhythm of my breathing. Just before unconsciousness again carried me off into its freeing oblivion, I heard the door close softly and, in my delirium, felt a strange and sudden fancy for Yorkshire pudding. Thus ended the month of April, not with a bang but a whim.

Changing Currents
May 1770

At the start of May, I found myself mulling over the notion of what it is in a man's spirit that compels him to leave home and family and sail away for long periods. I'd never given it much thought before, but as the quarrels on board worsened, I began to regret my decision to lead the expedition. It is well known that Alexander Dalrymple was considered the obvious choice as leader and principal observer. Dalrymple's credentials certainly stood him in good stead. He was a member of the honoured and ancient Dalrymple family of Scotland, holders of the earldom of Stair, and his life was a succession of achievements; a scholar, seafarer, humanitarian and Fellow of the Royal Society. Even *I* expected his appointment, considering that his privately published work, *An Historical Collection of the Several Voyages and Discoveries in the South Pacifick Ocean*, had given substance to the existence of the Southern Continent and that it was the Royal Society itself which had petitioned the Admiralty for another ship to be sent south. So when, on the 25th of May, 1768, the Admiralty promoted me to 1st lieutenant and gave me, James Cook, a forty-year-old Whitby seaman unknown in society, command of the *Endeavour*, none was more surprised than I.

The early morning of May 1st, grey and cold as ingratitude, was in stark contrast to the conditions and vista experienced only a few hours earlier. The previous evening we'd sailed, fully-rigged, into a most commanding bay. Keen to investigate the region, I then initiated a familiar procedure; "Helm hard to port. Boatswain, brace back the square sails. Have the men stand by the windlass. Steady as she goes, wait till she's stopped... steady... now, let go the anchors!"

The gently blinking stars and the marble-still sea allowed a fitful sleep until the wind blew up close to 6.30 a.m.. Joseph Banks had risen and gone ashore before the rest of us had woken, and just as I was emerging through the hatch after breakfast, the botanist returned to the ship with Herman Sporing, his sketch-maker. The chill of the early morning was gradually losing its edge as the sun's flush forced its way through the parting clouds. The warmth hadn't yet reached my spirit as I quizzed Banks about his unexplained absence. He mumbled something about going ashore and then gushed about the richness of the flora and fauna.

"Show the captain your sketches, Mr Sporing," he said finally, completely oblivious to the fact that his absence had caused a good deal of worry. I pushed the sketches away without looking and then reminded the botanist that whenever he left the ship, it was his duty to inform somebody.

"I did," Banks protested.

"Who?"

"Me," said Sporing.

There seemed little point in continuing the conversation, so I turned and surveyed all around. The region, with its deep anchorage, calm, blue waters and pleasant climate, created a sense of freedom from threat, and as we stood beside the mizzen-mast, with the breeze at our backs and our eyes upon the distant, tree-covered hills, Joseph was elated. He clapped his hands rapidly, like volleys from a line of muskets, and laughed like a lad as the echoes chased each other around the sweep of the bay.

"Only once before have I experienced such a feeling of freedom," he said, quickly adding that the area should be called *Escape Bay* after William Bay, the dissolute London magistrate. He then went on to say that it was Bay who had concealed his name and released him from responsibility during three dishonourable breach-of-promise suits during 1765.

"I thanked the magistrate in the tavern at the celebrations after the third trial," Banks said, "and I told him that it would have been embarrassing had my scent reached the running noses of the press-hounds. The beef-witted old lard basket nodded knowingly, patted my hand and said, 'My pleasure, Joseph. You know the old saying - a friend in need is a friend in debt.'"

"What was your response?"

"One appropriate to the legal fraternity; the price of a gin and the promise of another. So as we sat by the fire, I ordered a couple of drinks, mainly to become better acquainted with the serving girl, and when she placed the cups on the table, I was instantly taken with her big, blue eyes and the smell of burning pine logs in her hair. She flashed me a smile so I flashed back."

"Do you mean," I interrupted, "that the girl had pine logs burning in her hair?"

Joseph slapped his hand against the mast with an exaggerated flourish. "Yes, it did sound like that, but I meant that the smoke from the fire had permeated her hair."

I nodded my understanding and stiffened my legs as a swell lifted the anchored hull. Banks wrapped his arm around the mast for support, held up his index finger and said, "Now that you've raised the subject of writing, let me digress for a couple of minutes to tell you about a new technique I've been thinking about. In all the stories I've read, I've never seen one that depicts a person's thoughts as they really occur. You know, a never-ending, chaotic flow. So when I get back to England and accept a lucrative offer from one of the many publishers who will be clamouring for my brilliant account of the voyage, I'm going to record thoughts as they literally flow out. I've called it the 'Lake of Consciousness' technique."

The ship slid into a small hollow between swells. As it rose, I suggested that a lake, being peaceful, contradicted the notion of chaotically flowing thoughts. Another hollow and Banks braced himself. "Point taken. What about 'Ocean of Consciousness'?"

A carnation-white cloud hung in the sky above us like an adornment upon a blue velvet jacket. Parrots screeched in the trees behind the beach, startling the lorikeets which became a flurry of small, feathered rainbows.

"That's closer," I replied, licking the salt from my lips, "but the image of an ocean doesn't convey a concentrated flow. It's too expansive."

The botanist sniffed at the briny air, then, seized by an irrepressible flash of dullness, clapped his lily-white hands and said triumphantly, "'Sewer-pipe of Consciousness'!"

A long, frustrated sigh preceded my response. "Too much dysentery and not enough poetry. What do you think of 'Stream of Consciousness'?"

"Not much. I'll come up with something later. Anyway, let me finish my story about old Willy Bay. As he guzzled the last of his gin, his parting words to me were, 'Mr Banks, I've always maintained that the English system of justice, much like banks, insurance companies and parliament, is presided over by the finest gentlemen money can corrupt'."

There was no way I could let the botanist's cavalier attitude towards the law's due process pass without comment, so I reprimanded him for his apparent complicity in the affair. I then imposed my authority, both moral and legal, over him by declaring that the region should be called *Botany Bay* because of the abundant variety of botanical species sketched by Sporing. Joseph appeared to take my reprimand with equanimity, but later in the day, as he and I were in the Great Cabin discussing certain flora, he made it obvious that he harboured resentment.

The specimen under discussion was a large and ubiquitous tree that gave off a pungent, antiseptically pleasant, odour. It also yielded a large quantity of reddish gum. For that reason, and as a friendly suggestion, I proposed that it should be called the *Gum Tree*.

Banks' mouth twisted to a snarl and the atmosphere in front of his eyes iced as he replied, "Who's the renowned botanist and who's the sailor? You concentrate on steering this bucket of bolts and I'll name the plants."

The curtain on the cabin's window was half-drawn, enabling filigreed light to fall upon the desk and chair. Further away in the shadows, Banks and I stood no more than a contemptible sigh from each other, controlling our breathing as we tried to silently impose our respective wills. As captain, I was determined to win, but it quickly dawned on me that he might use my hard-headedness as the excuse needed to incite the crew to mutiny. Reluctantly I backed down and told him to call it whatever he wanted. He immediately became insufferable. Grinning like some Sunday School bully who'd just thrashed the vicar's kitten, he flung the door of the cabin open, stood in the passageway and announced loudly, "Gum Tree be damned! Listen, everyone, I predict that in years to come, the Great Southern Continent will be famous for one thing; the 'Oozing Red-Sap Tree', so named by me this moment!"

It was obvious that Banks was desperate to sign his name on the canvas of natural history and to have it hung in the museum of men's minds. The opposite was, and is, the case for me. When I die, I will be satisfied with an uncrowded farewell in a quiet country church and the words, 'He was an honourable man who set to sea for King and country'.

I pray that day is long in coming, for I want so much to see my children grown. I also pray that when that day comes, it comes as a feather and not as a falcon, because violent death is too cruel a fate.

For Forby Sutherland, the end came very early in the month, and although not violent, it was nonetheless painful. The able seaman died as a result of consumption and the general distress did little to lessen the tension. When it became obvious that Sutherland was nearing his end, I ordered Banks and his 'gentlemanly' companions to leave the Great Cabin, in which they often worked and prattled, and arranged for Sergeant Edgecumbe and four other marines to carry Sutherland to it. Surgeon Monkhouse attended him for several hours and then rested on the poop while Gore and I sat with the stricken seaman. We spoke for a long time about serious matters; good versus evil, repentance, salvation and the hope of eternal joy in the life to come. Sutherland's breath grew weaker and shallower, and his final words indicated a certain lack of stoicism.

"Captain," he gasped as he wrapped his thin arms tightly around my neck, "the thought of death has never troubled me but the actual dying's another matter altogether. I DON'T WANT TO GO!"

"If the poor bugger hadn't put so much effort into saying he didn't want to go," Gore whispered as he pressed the deceased's eyes shut, "he might've hung on a bit longer. So much for final wishes being respected."

After the customary medical examination, Surgeon Monkhouse confirmed Sutherland's death. Lieutenant Hicks, the officer attending the examination, was a little confused on this point.

"Sir," he said as we strolled sedately along the top deck at twilight, musing over life's brevity and gazing across the water at the purpling, distant mountains, "why did the surgeon say, 'Leave him, he stinks'? It struck me as rather callous."

"You need the wax removed from your ears, Mr Hicks. Monkhouse simply made the formal pronouncement, 'Life extinct'. "

There was no hint of embarrassment or apology in Hick's voice as he said, "It doesn't matter. Either way, Forby's stiff as a Stilton."

A passage from The Proverbs came to me; 'Leave the presence of a fool, for there you do not meet knowledge'. "Hicks, I'm going below. You wouldn't know suffering if it thrashed you with the anchor cable."

The lieutenant stopped abruptly beside the main hatch, blocking my access, and said testily, "That's unfair. I *am* familiar with suffering."

"Undoubtedly," I said as I pushed past, "but only as the cause, never the recipient."

The following day, just as the sun was climbing into the sky, charging the heavens with life-renewing heat and light, Sutherland was buried ashore. As the company was quietly leaving the burial site, Monkhouse approached me and Gore. The three of us stopped beneath the boughs of a River Oak, the dappled light sprinkling onto our heads like drops of water from a baptismal font. Birth and death together; promise and passing contained in the one melancholy moment.

"I regret not being with poor Sutherland when he died," Monkhouse whispered. "Was he peaceful at the end?"

"I'd say so," Gore interposed. "He wasn't moving."

In the interests of honest accounting, it is necessary for me to record that William Brougham Monkhouse, although literate and deserving of praise both as an observer and surgeon, was not without blemish. Before joining the *Endeavour* expedition, the surgeon had known Banks. In 1766 they had sailed together on the thirty-two-gun frigate *Niger* to Newfoundland. They did so to prevent serious conflict between French fishermen and our own three years after the Treaty of Paris had been signed at the end of the Seven Years War. It was on this expedition that Monkhouse had shown a fondness for the fortifier. He then carried it with him, in three barrels, when he joined the *Endeavour*.

On a number of occasions during the voyage I counselled the surgeon concerning the evils of drink and then during the afternoon of May the 6th, after I'd seen him reel from his small and poorly aired cabin aft on the lower deck, I escorted him up to the poop and told him that unless he freed himself from the grip of the grog, he'd spend the rest of the voyage unproductive, green-faced and leaning over some rail.

"Remind me about this conversation in a few minutes," Monkhouse mumbled as he hastily leaned over the stern. It was unfortunate that at the precise moment the doctor threw up, a nor'easterly blew up, and a few seconds later an enraged Banks propelled his sour krout-covered head through the opened window of the Great Cabin and shouted, "Monkhouse, you quack, if you're still on the deck when I reach it, you'll feel my boot up your Aylesbury arse!"

The doctor was coherent enough to realise he was in trouble, so he fled towards the men's fo'c's'le below. He stayed there for an hour or so, expecting to be battered and bloodied, but when it became apparent that Banks' ill-temper had been constrained less by his high-mindedness and more by his low cowardice, Monkhouse at last felt free to emerge.

For the next two days, things ran smoothly, so I was able to schedule necessary business. This concerned itself with frequent visits ashore with the treacherous botanist and his colleague, Dr Solander. These visits were necessary in order to inspect the remarkable variety of plant and animal life that flourished in Botany Bay. Even though my mind was alert to any danger, the walking gave me a welcomed break from the tensions aboard ship.

During all my years at sea, I have been fortunate to see many exceptional places. Botany Bay was another, and in many ways the most unusual. Apart from many species of eucalypts set back from the beach, there was also the River Oak with its huge, straight trunk and branches thick as a thigh. High above, its canopy was green, and the earth beneath, a chess board of light and shadow, was moist and fertile. Pines and palms crowded along the shore, their fronds bowing and rising in the breeze. At the head of the harbour, dark mangroves hid frogs, crabs and crows.

All this vegetation provided shelter for an array of other birds such as cockatoos, seagulls and pelicans. On one occasion when we noisily approached such a gathering, the alarmed flock flew with a flourish and became a white brushstroke across the blue canvas. I envied the strength of this display. Water fowls browsed and fed along the shore, and on the sand and mud flats we relished the sight and taste of oysters, cockles and mussels.

Another sight relished by the men, Banks in particular, was the native women. Whether they were fossicking along the beach, digging amongst the trees or carrying wood to their camps and huts, they seemed oblivious to the fact that they were naked and open to view. I called them 'brazenly immodest'. Solander termed them 'naturally charming'. Banks was rendered almost speechless and kept dousing himself with sea water. Not that it had much effect. I recall one day in particular; a stain in time that no amount of trinket-swapping could wipe away.

Solander, Banks, some waterers and I had gone ashore to collect fresh water and small life forms living on the rock platform. It was our final excursion before continuing up the coast, and after a morning's fruitful toil, the party climbed into the heavily laden long-boat and made ready the oars. Just as we were setting off, I noticed that Banks wasn't aboard. Being aware of the lurking dangers and of the botanist's ability to turn peace into problem with minimal effort, I told the waterers to stand by the boat while Solander and I searched him out. We'd walked only a short distance from the beach when we came across Banks and a group of women sitting in a circle in the shade of a large eucalypt. As usual, the women were naked, and Joseph was giving them each a shiny shilling and an even brighter smile. Annoyed at being delayed, I strode over and asked what he was up to.

"I'm trying to persuade these lovely young things to let me paint them," he said, eyeing-off the most voluptuous of the subjects.

Solander was immediately taken aback. Standing over his colleague and plunging him into even darker shadow, he said, "What with? You didn't bring your oils."

Banks, not taking his eyes off his intended prizes, replied, "They're going to show me how to make some using various coloured clays."

"And what about brushes?" Solander pressed.

"Who needs brushes? I was going to finger-paint."

I was as curious as Daniel. "But you haven't even brought a canvas."

Shaking his head impatiently, Joseph stood and dragged me to one side. "Mr Cook," he said, "I'm trying something radical here, so don't interfere. When I told you I wanted to paint the girls, especially that big one, I meant that I actually wanted to put the paint on them."

"Their faces?"

"Eventually, but I'd have to work up to it. And if you and Solander don't smother my genius with the wet blanket of your working-class outrage, I'll let you watch."

I grabbed his arm and pulled him back to the circle of girls. "Give them each another shilling but you keep the lecherous smile. Let's call it payment for services rendered redundant."

When they had their coins, I said, "Shoo," and waved them away with both hands. "And as for you, Joseph, I'll tell you what you can do with your fingers. Get back to the boat, wrap them around one of the oars and heave with all your carnal genius."

When we eventually reached the ship, I gave the order to weigh anchor. Banks, standing jelly-legged beside me on the poop, took a final look at a group of girls fishing near the shore, let out a long, deep sigh then took to his bed with the glazed expression of one who had lost contact with the world as we know it.

Once again in the safety of my own suite, I was relieved that no mishap had overtaken me or my men.

I was also confident that Banks' mutinous intent would remain dormant, considering his state of mind.

It was now the afternoon of the 7th and it seemed an appropriate time to check the suggestion box again. Just as I was opening it, Lieutenant Hicks arrived carrying two mugs of steaming tea. "I thought you could use a spot of refreshment," he said.

I commended him for his timing, beckoned him in, sat and asked him to read the papers aloud. The lieutenant positioned a chair on the other side of the desk, reached into the box, scanned the first paper and said, "This would definitely be well received, Captain, but I doubt that it'll work. There isn't enough fuel on board to boil oil and I can't see the boatswain agreeing to get into the barrel in the first place."

I told Hicks to put it in the over-flowing waste basket. After a further fifteen minutes of listening to a series of illiterate gripes, death threats and false accusations, only one suggestion remained.

"Don't bother reading it, Mr Hicks. I'm planning on abandoning this box in front of me and putting all these execrable papers behind me when I visit the head later."

Through the partly-opened window, a gentle nor'easterly brushed past my face and rustled the final suggestion in Hicks' fingers. He glanced at it then turned it towards the light filtering through the window.

"Not so fast, Sir," he said. "This one might just be the vindication you need. It starts off, 'Dear Captain Cook. Before I give you me idea I want to tell you that Mr Hicks is as popular as a fart in a flower shop'. Maybe

I was a bit too optimistic... let me skip down to the nub of this thing... here it is; 'entertainment evening'. It then mentions singing and acting... magic tricks... juggling. What do you think?"

It wasn't the type of activity which normally interested me, but I was seized by the notion that a night's entertainment might just be the tonic needed to lift the men's spirits. And more importantly, the resultant betterment might also provide a bulwark against any treachery Banks might seek to foster. After a minute's thought, I nodded my assent and Hicks clapped his hands together like a small, enthralled boy watching a Punch and Judy show on a seaside pier. He then asked me to fix a time for the event.

"Tomorrow night after mess," I said, "and you can hold it on the lower deck. It'll be too cramped to house the entire crew at one time so I want two shows. There's a lot to do so get cracking."

For the next 36 hours, a mood of excited expectancy washed over our sturdy ship as the men readied themselves for the show. Chores were hurriedly completed, not one shit-sack grumbled, and so it seemed that my decision had been already vindicated. When the appointed hour finally arrived, I gave the order to heave-to. The inlet I'd called *Port Stephens*, named after the only sailor on board desperate enough to drink the stuff, was a mile to the west and when I excused the men on evening watch, Able Seaman Stephens smiled broadly and slurred that all was well. His pleasure could barely be contained as he and the others jostled through the hatch, their laughter as full as the moon. The lights from the lower deck blazed through the opening, their brilliance thrusting and climbing all the way up the mainmast.

A head suddenly popped up through the hatch. "We're ready to start, Captain," Hicks said. "I've saved you a seat at the front."

The crewmen assigned to the second performance were stationed at various points along the upper deck and I told them to be patient and alert as I clambered down through the hatch. Upon reaching the lower deck, I saw that it had been arranged as a small theatre. Aft was a stage constructed from planks and supported at each corner by a barrel. Hanging in front of the stage was a curtain made from a torn sail. A line of lamps just under the stage threw up a dazzle of light and the smoke from the lamps filled the room with a yellow fog. Presently onto the stage stepped my 2nd lieutenant. He held up his arms and the audience hushed.

"Good evening. Gentlemen and Gentlemen," he announced, bowing grandly, "and welcome to what I know will be an unforgettable evening. For your pleasure, H.M.S. Endeavour would like to present, as the opening attraction, Dr Daniel Solander performing a slightly abridged rendition of the soliloquy from William Shakespeare's immortal work 'Hamlet'. Come on lads, put your hands together. Lads, you're being silly. Now part them. That's right. Now together again, apart, faster, faster. That's the spirit!"

A howl of encouragement almost blew the ballast through the hull. With a theatrical flourish, Solander pushed both the curtain and Hicks aside and waited for silence. He then cleared his throat and slowly raised the coconut he was holding until it was level with his widened eyes.

"Alas! Poor Youpricks," he boomed. "I knew… I knew… shit, I knew I'd forget what comes next. Can someone help me out?"

Jumping from his seat, John Gore yelled, "Allow me!" He then grabbed Solander by the scruff of his neck, yanked off his paper crown and helped him out through the hatch, arse first.

As soon as Gore returned to his seat, accompanied by cheers and acclamation from the entire audience, Hicks reappeared. "Thank you very much, Dr Slander! And now, good sirs, our next artiste is a man who needs no introduction."

"Then don't give the prick one!" Solander yelled jealously down the hatch.

"Right," Hicks responded. "Attraction number three. I'd like to give you a chap who…"

"We don't want him!" shouted the just-rejected number two.

"Number four it is then. Lads, I present Surgeon William Monkhouse singing that beautiful English ballad *I Asked My Lass for Her Hand in Marriage but All I Got Was The Finger*."

A quick roll from Drummer Rossiter was Monkhouse's signal. A few seconds ticked by without anything happening so Rossiter thumped his drum again. I was becoming as impatient as the rest when Hicks reappeared and said, "Sorry, Doctor Monkhouse won't be coming out. He's been on the grog and he's off his face. So while we're waiting for the next performer to get ready, I'd like to recite a poem that I wrote especially for tonight. It's in the style of the English Romantics. Here goes... James Cook stood on the quarter-deck, amid a storm quite dire. A lightning flash shot up his pants and set his arse on fire... oh, you're ready number five. Gentlemen, as a tribute to one of our ship-mates who recently passed away, Observer Charles Green would like to do his sensitive impression of the late Forby Sutherland."

Slowly the curtain slid apart. In the middle of the stage was a makeshift coffin with a stiff arm hanging out. The curtain then quietly closed.

Up to this point, the show hadn't been the rollicking good time I'd hoped for, but it was still early and I was still optimistic. Stretching my legs to relieve a minor cramp, I then looked up and saw James Magra standing in the middle of the stage.

"Evenin' all," he announced. "I'm 'ere to astound youse with me bird calls. Ready? HEY, YOUSE FUCKIN' STUPID BIRDS!... hahaha... come on, boys, there's no law against clappin'."

None of us responded to Magra's exhortation, so the curtain closed quickly and ten seconds later the infuriating Hicks was back. Much to my relief, it was at this point that Zachariah announced a short refreshment interval. Every man stood, most stretching their stiffened spines and massaging the backs of their legs. A moment or two later, Gastro appeared straight from the galley. He was carrying a small tray filled with chocolate-covered artichokes on sticks. "Artichocs," he called. "Get your artichocs here!" but before he had a chance to circulate, several crewmen hoisted him across their shoulders and carried him straight back to the galley, whereupon, I was later told, they force-fed him the artichocs *and* half the tray.

Apart from an opportunity to stretch our legs, the interval gave me, and a number of others, the chance to assess the performances we'd seen.

"I'm no critic," Charles Green commented, "but the most appealing parts of Solander's soliloquy were the brief silences between the words."

"Beggin' the Gentlemen's pardons," Peckover said, pushing between me and Green, "but I couldn't help overhearin' what you be sayin' and I'd just like to add a word of compliment for good ol' Mr 'icks. He be doin' a mighty fine job up front."

Banks placed his arm around Peckover's shoulder and said, "I'll say this for you, Seaman Prickowner. You're a keen judge of unrelenting mediocrity."

I could see the lieutenant waving eagerly at me from the stage, so I called for hush and told the men to sit down again. When the deck was relatively quiet, Zachariah tried his best to muster enthusiasm.

"Discerning patrons, may I introduce 'The Incredible Swami Orton and His Amazing Prestidigitations'! How about a round of applause?"

Two or three crewmen responded with minimal effort so Hicks tried a little harder. "A round of ammunition?"

A slightly more spirited reaction.

"A round of drinks?"

The entire audience erupted with all the force and fury of a Cape Horn tempest. It became annoyingly excessive, so I instructed the boatswain to call the men

PLOTS, CLOTS and CALAMITY | 95

to order. When they'd finally settled, my clerk, Richard Orton, strode into the middle of the stage with the goat's unwashed blanket wrapped around his body and a small dishcloth curled precariously on his head.

"Can I have a volunteer from the audience?" he asked. Master Molyneux immediately stood up.

"Anyone will do," Orton persisted.

The master waved his arms frantically, but Orton continued to ignore him. "Oh, well," the Swami shrugged, "I'll just have to choose. How about that chap in the third row?"

A ferocity of forearms pushed Able Seaman Dozey forward. "Good evening, complete stranger," Orton said as Dozey joined him on stage. "I'd like you to confirm for the audience the fact that we haven't met before."

Dozey looked directly at me. "He's wrong, Skipper. Me and him have been practisin' this trick all frickin' day."

"Hahaha...very amusing. Now, unknown volunteer," Orton moaned mystically as he held up a deck of cards, "I want you to choose one of these cards and commit it to memory. Then I want you to slip it back in the deck. I will then shuffle the deck and select the card you chose."

Dozey nodded his understanding and Orton fanned out the cards. "Choose any card... no, any card but that... or *that*. Take the one near my finger... not **that** finger! The one with the ring. Good grief, can't you do *anything* right? Take the card with the bloody big red cross on it!"

Like the rest of us, Lieutenant Gore's patience had run out. From his seat in the front, he shouted, "Orton, you've got all the skill of a one-armed juggler. Get off and take dumb-arse Dozey with you!"

Several of the audience took this as their cue to voice their own judgements, with expressions such as 'cut his bloody throat, not the cards', 'Orton the Bloody Ordinary' and 'let's see the Swami swim' being common and seriously intended. Realising that a nasty incident was in the making, the 2nd lieutenant rushed onto the stage and attempted to restore peace. He failed, so during a momentary lull in the cat-calling, I stood and told the men to shut up or else the show would stop there and then. I secretly hoped that they'd continue their uproar so that I could call the wretched thing off, but when they hushed almost immediately, I was obliged to let it continue. My nod to Hicks indicated as such.

"Thank you. Now comes the 'piss de assistants', as the French say. Would you please welcome Able Seaman Thomas Matthews and His Troupe of Performing Field-Mice! Take us out, Thomas!"

With a stuttering, uncertain movement, the curtain opened and there stood Matthews juggling three of the biggest rats ever seen outside the Paris sewer system. One after the other they circled in the air and one after the other they dropped to the floor.

"Kill the frigging lights!" Hicks shouted in a state of sheer panic.

"Kill fucking Matthews!" Gore screamed, jumping onto his chair. Immediately, the entire audience followed his example.

From the stage, Matthews' voice pierced the darkness. "A standin' ovation! Gosh! I never expected nuffink like this!"

An eerie silence then fell upon the lower deck, punctuated at intervals by the sounds of rabid gnawing. Apparently convinced that the men were too preoccupied with their own safety to wreak any further havoc, Hicks stumbled his way back to the stage and said, "That's it. Have you all had fun? Mr Gore, can we have a light on the audience? That's better... oh, there's no audience."

It came as no surprise that I cancelled the second show and ordered everyone to his cabin or hammock. Everyone except Zachariah Hicks. He was to wait for me on the quarter-deck. It was time for a talk.

When the men were settled, I went atop. The sky and sea merged into a vast, black cape wrapped loosely around the ship, allowing the water-cooled wind to bully its way along the deck and into my bones. Hicks was standing on the poop, rubbing his hands. As I approached, he stiffened. His mouth then opened, a puff of frosty air preceding the words he was about to utter. My hand went up and his mouth closed.

"Lieutenant," I said coldly, "tonight was a disaster. I'd trusted you to organise an evening that reflected English life at its best; Sunday on the village green with its vaulters, minstrels and morris-dancers. But what did I see? A pig-awful procession of bad acting, insults, insubordination and even violence. All that was missing were cock-fights and bear-baiting. I was hoping for fond memories and lasting goodwill. Fat chance!"

Throughout my harangue, Hicks stood motionless, his head bowed.

"It's no wonder you lack the courage to look me in the eye. If Gore were more trustworthy, I'd reduce you to 3rd lieutenant and promote him to 2nd. But that'd be like putting my left foot inside my right boot, just for the sake of a change. I'll continue to wear you till my patience gives out but any more slip-ups and you'll wish you'd never been born. Is that understood?"

He nodded. I then headed for the hatch and my bed, ordering him to stand night-watch for the next two days so that he could reflect on his position. It must have been close to 3 a.m. before the fog of sleep drifted from the water and filled my cabin.

For the next few days, with their variable light winds and clear weather, we continued our voyage. Our course was due north, and we maintained a distance of some two or three miles from land. In these warmer waters, dolphins often surfaced and swam beside the ship, their snouts playfully pushing through the swells. To port, the coast was a changeable, yet all the time, compelling, attraction. One day showed it to be a line of white sand with flat, stumpy trees behind, the next saw cliffs rising out of the emerald water like sunburnt icebergs. Never more obvious was the variety of Nature's handiwork, inspiring awe with the intake of every breath.

Sanguine as my mood appeared, the men knew only too well that I would not react well to any further provocation, so it wasn't surprising that the external calm carried itself into the *Endeavour*. Given this truce, I allowed myself a day to inspect the ship without interruption. Considering she'd been at sea for almost two years, she was in a state of reasonably good repair. I could detect little fault with her masts, spars, standing and running rigging or her sails, and the caulking on the decks and upper works was sound. The lower hold, filled with barrels, casks and provisions, was dry, as were the carpenters' workshop, sail-lockers, pantries, cabins and magazines. I was at ease with the ship and grateful that her refitting at Deptford had been so thorough, and just as I was beginning to feel that Banks' covert machinations might be rendered impotent, Fate stuck out its foot again and I tripped.

At near to 11 on the morning of May the 14th, as I was inspecting the deck which had been built in the hold to provide slinging room for the seamen's hammocks, Sergeant Edgecumbe and two other marines approached me. They had a problem with my clerk, Richard Orton. Edgecumbe had been appointed spokesman and he wasted no time in establishing his position.

"Sir," he said, stepping in front of the others, "last night in the carpenters' workshop, Orton taught a few of us a game he'd picked up from a traveller returned from the Americas in 1767. He called it 'poker'."

"Yes, I know it... similar to the European game, 'poque'. So what's the problem?"

Edgecumbe glanced at his mates. They both nodded their permission.

"Well, we're pretty sure the bastard cheated."

"How do you know?"

"He gave us five cards each."

"That's how many you're supposed to get."

"So why'd he give himself seven?"

"Perhaps he miscounted."

"The only thing he miscounted on was in thinkin' we couldn't count past five."

"That was probably the safest bet of the night."

"Excuse me?"

"I said you should feel safe letting this problem come to light."

"See?" Edgecumbe said to his companions. "I told you the cap'n would understand. We want the swindlin' shyte to give us our money back."

Having listened to this sorry tale, I had to be seen to be impartial and in total command. There were two reasons. First, I had authority over men whose moral fibre was well and truly moth-eaten, and unless I acted with conviction, our small society was in danger of coming apart at the seams. Second, if I failed to comply with naval regulations, Banks' mutinous intentions would be given fuel. I therefore resolved to administer immediate discipline to my clerk. Rather than send for him, I determined to search him out myself. No delegation, no second-hand messages that might cause misunderstanding. Just the captain and the culprit. The news of the encounter would soon spread anyway.

He wasn't in his cabin or the mess so I went up to the main deck. A short but heavy rain storm had just stopped and the air was still and moist. Half a dozen gulls had settled on the spritsail-yard and they were watching the rain-flattened sea for the slightest movement of fish. On the shoreline about a mile distant, just south of *Cape Byron*, thin, white lines curled upwards. The natives were re-lighting their fires that the rain had doused. It took little time for the smoke, drifting through the grey air like a spirit, to reach the ship. I inhaled deeply and was pleased because it was a reminder of family life. Often I'd lit the fire at home. Elizabeth would then stitch, I would read and the boys would play. Elizabeth would occasionally look down at the boys, then across to me, and smile. I knew the contents of her heart by the contentment in her eyes. After a time the fire would fade, so I'd add another log. This was the pattern that gave my life its limited joy; my family and I, sitting together around the fire, not needing to speak.

Suddenly one of the gulls squawked as a fish darted and I was cruelly brought back to the ship and my purpose. As we moved through the water at a steady five knots, I stepped carefully across the slippery deck and looked towards the mizzen-mast. There the accused was, leaning against it in a stupor. He didn't see me coming, but he looked up wearily when I said, "Orton, you've let me down."

He started sobbing, a response that made my stomach churn, so I wasted no time in applying my saltiness to the weeping wound that wobbled in front of me. In the space of thirty seconds, I rattled off his deficiencies, the names of his enemies and the charges laid against him. After he'd slurringly admitted his guilt, I ordered him to repay those whom he'd cheated.

I assumed, incorrectly as it turned out, that this would placate his victims. It didn't, because two days later, while he was sleeping in his cabin during the middle watch, someone crept in and cut off a part of both his ears. The culprit responsible for the knife attack remained at large until word eventually reached me that James Magra was somehow involved, so I summoned Hicks and Gore to my suite to discuss the matter. Both felt that the reasons for suspecting him were insubstantial. For the sake of justice, I listened as the 2nd lieutenant attempted to refute them.

"Let's consider the first reason," he said, rising from his chair with his hands clasped behind his back. "Magra can't account for his movements at the time of the assault. So what? John, can you account for yours?"

Gore was forceful in his own defence. "Absolutely. I was asleep."

"Any witnesses?" Hicks demanded, his interrogatory finger an exclamation mark.

"Only one. While I was out to it, I dreamed I was eating jellied eels on Blackpool Beach with the Archbishop of Canterbury. We then swapped hats and paddled with our trousers rolled up. He'll vouch for me."

A few seconds of strained silence elapsed before my patience finally snapped. "Mr Gore," I barked, "the vacivity of your head is in stark contrast to the quantity of crackbrained conversation it generates. Gentlemen, let's just consider the facts. Zachariah, I'm prepared to admit that the evidence relating to Magra's whereabouts is open to conjecture, but surely the second reason for suspicion carries weight?"

Hicks' voice was reed-thin and reserved. "Perhaps."

My voice was wind-wild. "Perhaps! Eighty-three men clearly heard Magra say to Orton, 'You're a dirty cheat so one of these nights I'm going to cut off your ears', and yet you're still willing to defend him? I can't believe it! You're nothing but a boorish egotist who delights in the sound of his own voice."

"That's right. I'm pretending to be a lawyer."

"You're a louse," Gore growled, unaware that he had confirmed, rather than corrected, Hicks' statement.

Rising from my chair, I curtly dismissed them both and told Hicks to send Magra down. Following their departure, peace fluttered like a dove in the cabin. I closed my eyes and regulated my breathing. Then a loud rapping snapped me to attention. The door opened. It was Magra. He stood like a marble Grenadier in front of my desk and asked why I'd sent for him. My response was an accusing stare.

Unnerved, the midshipman said, "I 'spose it's about the attack on Mr Orton. Honest, Cap'n, I never laid a finger on 'im."

As the ship lurched, he steadied himself on the corner of the desk. Through the open window, I could hear the boatswain barking out orders to the men on the main deck. I closed the window and his voice was no longer a distraction.

"Midshipman Magra," I said, tapping my finger on the desk in time with the rhythm of my words, "did you say to Orton, 'You're a dirty cheat so one of these nights I'm going to cut off your ears'?"

A laugh of disbelief erupted from him. He then adopted a look of outrage and said, "No, Mr Cook. What I said was 'It bleats and one of these nights it's goin' to butt all our rears'. I were talkin' about the goat."

"That's ridiculous."

"I know, but it's the best I could come up with on such short notice."

The heat and tension inside the cabin were stifling, so I opened the window. Fresh air and the boatswain's voice from above again flooded in. "Hey, Dozey! When I told you to stand by the spanker, I meant the sail on the aft side of the mizzen-mast. So would you stop smacking Observer Green with that bloody great plank and do what I told you!"

I slammed the window shut and stood directly in front of Magra. Furious at being constantly at war with almost everyone on board, the ball of my words exploded from the cannon of my mouth.

"Up straight, no lies, you did it!"

His knees buckled under the force, and the recoil of his reply was immediate.

"Yeah, but 'e made me do it. Durin' the game, Orton said I didn't have enough nouse to put together a two-piece jigsaw, so I just seen red and sweared in me own mind to get even with 'im."

My eyes remained fixed on the reprobate as I relieved him of all duties. The midshipman produced a premature smile and said, "Fair 'nough. I'll be goin' now then."

"Not quite yet," I replied as I strode to the window, opened it and shouted for the boatswain to report on the double. When he appeared a moment later, I ordered him to escort Magra to the main deck.

"Don't go to all that bother," he interrupted. "I know where it is. I can toddle off by meself."

"Maybe so," I said, "but I doubt you'll be willing to give yourself ten lashes when you get there. Take him away, Mr Gathrey, and see that it's done."

Ten minutes later, as I stood by the opened window with my eyes focused on the promontory I called *Point Danger*, the swish of the whip on warm, bare flesh cut the air. It was chilling. Above the hills that passed across the corner of the frame, clouds were gathering. Beneath the stern, the sea churned and was black. Winds began to howl their fury against ropes and canvas. The *Endeavour* was being driven into a storm.

I felt its early rumblings about an hour after concluding the meeting with Magra. Wanting to check on our provisions, I went below. Just as I was entering the hold, Joseph Banks emerged carrying several sheets of paper. When he saw me, his face reddened and he quickly stuffed the papers inside his waistcoat.

"What's that?" I asked casually.

Banks feigned confusion. "Where?"

"In your waistcoat."

"That's my shirt."

"What are those papers?"

"Oh, these," he said, stuffing them deeper into his waistcoat. "They're just some idle scribblings about the things I saw when we were anchored in Botany Bay."

One or two timbers creaked as the ship listed. Banks swallowed hard. My resolve stiffened.

"Making notes in the hold, Mr Banks? A bit secretive, wouldn't you say? It's as if you've got something to hide."

A hollow laugh rang out. "That's absurd. I'm leaving."

I wasn't going to be put off. Here was my opportunity to catch Joseph in the process of organising the mutiny and I was determined to bring his scheme to light. "Can I see them?"

A frown appeared on Banks' forehead. He began to shuffle uneasily. "You wouldn't understand all the Latin names for the shrubs."

It would have been injudicious to accuse Banks of disloyalty without the evidence of his notes, so I demanded to see them. Like two slugs sliding, Banks' thumb and index finger slowly produced the papers. My eyes travelled at a similar pace down his face and shirt before finally coming to rest on the sheets. I took them and began reading;

'Botany Bay... Eucalyptus globulus... colourful parrots... native girls... fresh water... naked... oysters... flat stomachs... stretches of white sand... curves of brown skin... legs... cowrie shells... breasts like mangoes... thighs... bouncing and bending... finger-painting... no pirates off shore... lots of jolly rogering on shore...'

This wasn't the self-incrimination I'd anticipated, so direct confrontation was out of the question. However, to indicate that I suspected him, I crumpled the papers inside my fist and handed the tight ball back with the words, "Consider your position carefully."

"I always do," he said as he scurried up the narrow steps, "because experience has taught me that 'missionary' is less stressful on my back than either 'reverse milk maid' or 'stand and deliver'."

Before I had a chance to respond, he was gone. Quietness now inhabited the hold. Beside me was a barrel that contained a provision covered by a greenish sludge. As I was staring at it, Gastro came in and looked around. When he saw the barrel, he smiled. I decided to skip mess that evening, instead spending the time in my cabin scheduling the activities for the remainder of the month.

As a result of overhearing Dozey's misunderstanding of the word 'spanker', and in order to divert my thoughts away from Banks, I decided that the first activity should be a thorough reappraisal of the men's naval knowledge. After almost two years at sea, it was becoming apparent that their grasp of fundamentals was weakening. The problem needed to be corrected, so following the afternoon watch on the 22nd, I met with the boatswain in my cabin and told him to prepare a written examination.

"Make it a searching test, Mr Gathrey. In order to correct any deficiencies, I must first know where they lie."

"You'll catch most of the lazy bastards lyin' down in the hold," he said, standing to attention in front of the desk.

I took a deep breath and explained that I wanted a test of about ten questions on various masts, yards, rigging and sailing manoeuvres. It was to be done by the men after mess that night and the results brought to my cabin later for review.

It was close to midnight when Gathrey knocked on my door and announced he had the completed test papers. I was happy to call him in because it gave me a break from my charting.

"I've had a quick look," he said, placing the papers on top of the maps, "and considerin' the lateness of the hour, the men done pretty good."

Standing up to relieve the back strain from prolonged drawing, I asked if he'd encountered any problems.

"None to speak of. There was a minor kerfuffle when Matthews discovered that he hadn't brung a pencil so he lent one from Satterley. So then Satterley didn't have a pencil so he asked Tupia for one but he couldn't read a word so he pissed off. So Molyneux waited for Satterley to finish using Matthews' and they started arguing and then most of the other duck-fuckers joined the ruckus and..."

I was outraged. "I beg your pardon! What did you call them?"

"Same as you would've. I called 'em to order and the duck-fuckers shut up."

There was no point in pursuing my concern over his language so I simply said, "Enough, Mr Gore. I get the picture. Apart from the pencils, were there any other difficulties?"

"Only the time it took 'em to finish. Five hours."

"Five hours! How many questions were there?"

"Ten."

"That's ridiculous. Either your questions were too involved or the men are appallingly slow writers. Which is it?"

Gathrey was quick to spring to both his and the men's defence. "Neither. There was only one fuckin' pencil so they all had to take turns usin' it."

To relieve the tension building in my neck, I hunched my shoulders and rotated my head. "Was there any cheating?" I asked as I massaged my temples.

"Not much, although I did catch Pickersgill sneakin' a look at Sergeant Edgecumbe's answers so I fetched him a pencil and told him do the test by 'imself in the fo'c's'le."

"How did he fare?"

Gathrey shrugged his own shoulders and held his hands out sideways. "Buggered if I know. He's still wanderin' around the ship searchin' for it."

Feeling uneasy about Gathrey's earlier assessment, I again asked if the test had been thorough. The boatswain's fingers gripped the papers tightly and he said reassuringly, "Too right. Here, see for y'self."

He released his grasp, randomly extracted one of the papers, handed it to me then continued, "Mind you, with only one pencil, I had t' think on me dew beaters, so I read the questions out loud to each man when it was his turn and he writ 'em down and underlined 'em. Then he scribbled his answers beneath each one. When he was done, I got 'im to sign 'is names on the back of the sheet."

I congratulated Gathrey on a job well fucked up, settled comfortably next to the lantern and, in the dim light, focused my tired eyes on the paper. The first element that impressed me was the neatness of the setting out.

'Naval Examination
H.M.S. Endeavour
22nd of May
In the Year 1770

Question 1. Name two things that are kept in the magazine?
Shot and powder are kept in the magazine.
Question 2. What is a 'hawser'?
A hawser is a heavy rope for moorin' or haulin' the ship.'

Two questions and two correct answers! This was a promising start and my eyes eagerly moved down.

'**Question 3.** What does the term 'cast off' mean?
Cast off means the moth-eaten vest Dr Solander gave to the clothing collection for Tupia.

Question 4. What is the 'quarter-deck' and where is it located?
The quarter-deck is the number of cards Mr Orton deals himself when we're playing poker and the miserable shyte keeps it up his sleeve.

Question 5. Who is responsible for the rigging?
Mr Orton is responsible for the rigging and if we catch the bastard at it again, we'll tear up his crooked cards, open his bone box and shove them down his gutter lane.

Question 6. What is a 'crew'?
A crew is a type of piss-poor haircut worn by the marines.

Question 7. Define the term 'fother'.
He married my mather, and before you say anything, the ceremony took place **before** I was born.

Question 8. Where is the 'mess'?
Try the quartermaster's cabin, if you can get the fat pig's door open.

Question 9. Explain the word 'fathom'.
I've tried but I can't work it out.

Question 10. If you were an officer, under what circumstances would you expect to have your rank reduced?
After my monthly scrubbing with soap in a tub but I'm not sharing it with Peckover again. When he farts, little bubbles come up and he pops 'em with his nose.'

Despondently, I asked whose paper it was. The boatswain gestured for me to turn it over. A faint signature was scribbled in the bottom, left-hand corner.

"John Thompson! I might have guessed. Judging by this, it's a miracle that he knows the difference between a pot and a pelican. I'd actually considered giving him a break away from the galley, for his own welfare, but for ours, he can stay."

Never had twenty-four hours seemed so long and never had Mile End seemed so far away. Much closer was the bunk in the corner of the cabin, its blankets almost beckoning. Out of sheer frustration and weariness, I held Thompson's paper over the lantern's flame and watched, mesmerised, as it fulminated. The sparks rose then cascaded onto the baize. A thousand small insects fluttered against the cabin window, attracted by the little lights flittering in the room. Panic-stricken, Gathrey stamped out the embers, sat in my chair and then asked what my plans were.

"I'm not sure long-term," I replied, "but there's something I need to do now. See that pitcher of water near you on my desk? Give it to me."

"And the glass?"

"No," I said as I poured the pitcher's entire contents over Gathrey's smouldering hair. His initial shocked gasp soon turned to gratitude so he shook my hand and smiled. I returned his smile, not as an amiable response but because I noticed that his left eyebrow was singed and his right was missing. Wearied by yet another dismal event, I sat on my bunk and removed my boots. Gathrey, aware that he was the cause of my exasperation, shuffled uneasily before asking, "Captain, is there anything you need?"

"There is something you can get," I replied as my left boot flew past his blistered head. "OUT OF MY BLOODY SIGHT!"

There seemed little purpose in scheduling any activity designed to increase the men's seafaring knowledge, so during the latter days of May I concentrated on more physical pursuits such as visits ashore. For the most part they were concerned with studying the indigenous fauna.

In the p.m. of the 24th, being anchored in the Latitude 23°53'South, Dr Solander requested that I, Lieutenant Gore and young Sydney Parkinson accompany him ashore to survey and sketch the local birds. I wasn't keen to leave the ship, desiring instead to remain aboard to keep an eye on Banks. However, the young Parkinson, eager to fulfil his draughting commission, kept on at me, so I reluctantly agreed to the trip.

Sydney Parkinson was a persuasive advocate for his profession. He'd been recommended for the great undertaking by Banks, having earlier been introduced to Joseph by the nurseryman, James Lee. Parkinson was well-suited to Banks' party, being amiable, handsome, talented beyond his years, articulate and diligent. His only flaw, according to Joseph, was that he was from Edinburgh.

"But don't think too harshly of the lad," Solander advised Banks early in the voyage. "The fact that he's *from* Edinburgh and not *in* Edinburgh indicates a degree of intelligence not readily discerned in the usual Scot."

Having acceded to Solander's wish, we made off in the yawl and were not long in landing. Parkinson gathered his paints and sketch pads, Solander gathered his telescope, while I instructed Gore to gather his wits and watch for any signs of trouble from the natives. We then scaled a large hill. On reaching the summit, a breath-taking panorama stretched out below. For as far as the eye could see, hundreds of birds crammed the sky; gulls, cormorants, ducks and pelicans, all screeching and squawking. Suddenly, as if seized by a fit, Solander went rigid. "Look down there," he whispered, staring at a group of trees near the base of the hill. We hurriedly followed the line of his eyes and saw millions of truly wonderful butterflies smothering the foliage; velvet black wings turning blue near the edges, and underneath two vivid red spots.

"A flutter of lashes in the eye-blue sky," Parkinson pronounced poetically. A second later, and much to the lad's distress, a large bustard flew over and dumped its whitish waste on top of his black hair.

"What a shitty day thanks to that filthy bastard!" he yelled.

"What was that?" I asked.

Fearful of being reprimanded, Parkinson quickly modified his unseemly observation. "I said it would be fitting if we called this bay after the bustard."

"Then 'Bustard Bay' it is," I said, leading the party back down the hill. As we walked, the sun beat upon our backs and the humidity drenched our shirts. To minimise weariness, we moved slowly and after a time I became aware of an imperceptible change all around. No bird screeched, no insect droned, no animal rushed. The only challenges for my senses were the antiseptic smell of the bush and the under-breath of wind through grass. I stopped and sat, lost in the whispering, and recalled with affection my early years spent with my family on Thomas Skottowe's farm at Great Ayton in Yorkshire, near the village of Marton.

My father had been made foreman to Skottowe when I was eight, and even though our cottage was usually peaceful, there were unhappy moments. Sometimes, when Father would sit after our evening meal and talk, his voice would quieten as he realised that his hopes for a life marked by distinction were now futile. It was from these infrequent times that I determined not to repeat my father's mistakes, so whenever I wasn't needed to labour or attend the Postage School at Ayton, I would wander over the cold Cleveland hills, an explorer within the continents of my own imaginings, travelling miles and years in a single afternoon. Even our farm's name, *Fairyholme*, had a lightness that seemed to lift me away each time I whispered it. I was hearing it again now, more than thirty years later, on this afternoon in a continent of my own finding, yet my imaginings had brought me back to Ayton. I couldn't help but smile, and it occurred to me that life's happiness, in significant measure, issues from one's recollections and their irony.

As I slowly awoke from my reverie, I began to sense a menace lingering in the shadows. Gore thought it was my imagination playing tricks, so he disappeared into a thicket to show that all was well. Five seconds later he emerged walking backwards with a native's spear prodding him in the guts. Twelve more natives quickly appeared, their dark faces adorned with red and yellow dyes, their eyes white and wide.

Solander muttered an unintelligible Swedish oath while Parkinson, displaying the spirit common to 'gentlemen', leapt behind a large, sandstone rock and whimpered. I stood my ground and ordered Gore to stand his. Gore shouted that his was about a mile away and took off. He froze when a spear impaled his hat on the trunk of a eucalypt. Then young Parkinson, in a moment of inspired self-preservation, stood up, seized his paints and quickly applied stripes to each of our faces. We soon resembled our attackers, so the natives, in some sort of brotherly gesture, put down their weapons and welcomed us into their tribe. We socialised for more than an hour, exchanging trinkets then ideas on how best to start a fire. The natives demonstrated their technique first, rotating a thin piece of hardwood against some balsa until it eventually ignited. To increase its intensity, one of them blew gently on the smouldering ashes.

Solander then showed his method. He struck a match and his shirt sleeve instantly caught alight, so he tore it off at the shoulder seam and stamped on it. He then blew vigorously on his arm to cool it.

"I don't think you presented civilization in the best light," Gore said as we sat down to eat. A type of yam was passed around, and when one reached Parkinson, he said 'Yum' and popped it in his mouth. A few seconds later he muttered 'Yuck' and spat it out. The period between the yam's acceptance and the 'yum' had been friendly. Not so the pause following the 'yuck' and spit. Understandably, the natives took Parkinson's reaction to be an insult so they reached for their spears. Shaking his head and wagging his finger, Gore then reached for his musket. To the native chief's credit, he quickly reached the conclusion that his fire-power wasn't equal to ours, so he, too, muttered 'Yuck' and spat his yam out. His tribesmen did the same, prompting Solander to do likewise.

"A bond of friendship's been formed," the naturalist said, and for the next five minutes he and the natives spat at each other.

We were then invited to watch a spirited dance where our hosts impersonated several indigenous animals. Sticks were beaten together as accompanying rhythm for a long, hollow, blowing instrument, and under the blazing sun, the chief wailed as his men spun around, their legs lifted in exaggerated fashion. Gore was so taken by the mood that he jumped up and joined in. He looked like some sort of disjointed stick-insect running across hot coals. Unfortunately, he got carried away and unknowingly kicked the chief in the testicles. Down the warrior went, eyes watering, hands clutching crotch, wailing louder than ever.

"Is that part of the dance?" Gore asked as he rejoined us in our small circle.

"If it is," Parkinson replied, "then I'll play the wallflower."

When the chief finally stopped rolling around in the dirt, he crawled over to his companions. I could hear guttural hisses and whispers rising into a sort of chant, and before I had a chance to warn my men, the natives were on us, punching, thumping and biting. In the ensuing melee, the chief fell against the musket, causing it to let loose several pellets into his backside. Down he went again, shrieking and clutching his arse like some horse-faced baroness who'd just been goosed by the gardener.

It was the chance I'd been hoping for. Grabbing what I could of our equipment, I told everyone to head for the yawl. We ran for almost thirty minutes, looking over our shoulders, anticipating a spear in the back. None came, and it was a tremendous relief to find ourselves rowing towards the ship with only minor abrasions. Later that evening, after Parkinson had retired exhausted to his quarters, Hicks, I and a couple of midshipmen sat in the Great Cabin discussing the day's events.

Pouring a dollop of goat's milk into my coffee, I mentioned that Parkinson's quick thinking in relation to the paint showed a rare, life-saving ingenuity. Hicks passed me the sugar and suggested that Parkinson should be rewarded with a nightshirt from the King when we returned to England. I thought he'd meant knighthood and said so.

"No," the lieutenant insisted. "Nightshirt it was. We've all seen him sleep-walking and none of us can stand his East-London habit of kipping in his vest and torn underdrawers."

As the others laughed, I smiled tiredly, finished my coffee then ordered everyone to bed.

At 6 the next morning, the sun's rays streamed in through the window, erasing the smudge of the night. I rose, washed, dressed then went below to supervise the crew's breakfast. It passed without incident, only because the men refused to eat it, and the swabbing of the decks was also carried out peacefully. Then later, after the dismissal of the morning watch, I decided to check the suggestion box. There was only one proposal. It read;

'Dear Captain,

Like you, I'm a Christian, but no-one else gives a toss for spiritual matters. Apart from all of them being

real keen on sin. To make the men more God-fearing, could you please give some sermons and bible study? But steer clear of the arm-waving, fainting, scurvy-healing 'Pastor Jim' business that seems to be the fashion in the Americas just now. We're Englishmen, and nothing excites us. Straight and simple, that's the go.
God bless you, Captain.'

It was a positive and timely notion, giving me, as it were, the chance to kill two birds with one stone. The men's spiritual understanding could be developed, allowing them, when the time came, to choose between joining Banks' plotted treachery or submitting to my authority. With careful planning and execution, the odds could be stacked firmly in my favour. I rejected the thought of giving the sermon myself, feeling that it would simply be another example of a captain lecturing his wayward crew. The effect would be contrary to the intent, so I decided that Surgeon Monkhouse and Quartermaster Evans should lead the service.

A day of preparation followed. Monkhouse and Evans were advised as to what I expected, and on the morning of the 27th, being in the Longitude 22°53'South and becalmed, the boatswain had the crew assemble on the main deck. As I stood at the bow, gazing over the lads' heads and beyond to the stern, *Cape Manifold* reared up at a distance of almost ten miles. Its greenly rolling hills confirmed a complex, Higher Goodness at work. Hence the name. Surgeon Monkhouse was on the poop, watching for my signal. When he saw me nod, he took a step forward and said to the crew, "Good morning, brothers and brothers. Before I talk about how a personal relationship with the Lord can result in harmony with each other, Quartermaster Evans will lead us in a word of prayer."

Evans straightened, cleared his throat, and adopted a holier-than-thou expression. "Right, eyes closed and heads bowed. Almighty God in Heaven, we beseech Thee...Tupia, I can see you down there... stop peekin'!... to speak through Thy servant, Doctor Monkhouse, but please keep it short. Amen."

A loud 'Amen' echoed from the ranks. Monkhouse opened his eyes and gazed around. Like me, he saw that a few of the men were missing, so he asked the boatswain to do a head count.

"Twenty-five short," Gathrey reported.

"Go and get them," Monkhouse ordered. Biting my tongue, I watched as the reluctants filed up through the main hatch a minute or two later and joined the others in the ranks. Monkhouse was keen to prove himself worthy of my trust, so he held up his bible and said, "The text for today is taken from Saint Matthew, chapter eighteen, verse twenty. Able Seaman Dozey will now come up and read the verse."

Dozey then pushed his way through the ranks and Monkhouse handed him the Scriptures as he stepped onto the poop. He read the verse, returned the bible to the doctor then jostled back to his position.

"You were supposed to read it *aloud*, dumb-arse!" Monkhouse groaned. "Lads, it says, 'For where two or three are gathered together in my name, there am I in the midst of them'. This means that God Himself is on deck with us."

Immediately an arm shot up in the middle of the ranks. "Beggin' the Doctor's pardon, but if God be on deck with us, then who be watchin' over 'eaven to make sure no undesirables sneak in and grog-on like?"

Monkhouse turned his head towards the smoke that was rising on the shore-line two leagues away and took a deep breath. Having regained his composure, he turned back and said, "Peckover, God is omnipresent."

"No He ain't," the pestiferous seaman shouted. "God be a Roamin' Cathoholic."

Evans shot a glance in my direction, noticed my frown, then called for quiet. A sigh of gratitude preceded Monkhouse's words. "Thank you, Quartermaster. Men, to enter Heaven, we must first repent of our sin. Who knows what that means?"

In order to be heard above the squawks of several mast-perching gulls, my clerk, Charles Orton, called out, "It means to do the sin over and over again."

"Close," Monkhouse encouraged, "but you're confusing 'repenting' with 'repeating'."

Charles cupped what remained of his right ear and said, "I didn't hear a word of that. Would you mind repenting it?"

Even if I'd been on the shore two miles away, a wish that had fleetingly crossed my mind, I still would have heard the doctor's furious 'Shut the fuck up!' explode across the rippling water. But to his credit, he quickly apologised to the men and suggested that he, too, needed to repent. He then urged everyone to practise forgiveness by turning to someone and greeting him like a brother.

Peckover's arm went up again. "But what if we be orphans like, or only-children?"

Peals of ridiculing laughter swept through the ranks until Quartermaster Evans put an end to it by threatening to bring out the lash. Silence fell. Acting on his own initiative, a surprising yet welcomed development, Monkhouse then announced that a collection would be taken up in place of the sermon, adding, as a gentle reminder, that the Lord loved a cheerful giver. As an example to follow, he took a sovereign from his pocket and deposited it into the quartermaster's hat. Evans then ventured into the ranks. Two minutes later he returned and handed the hat to Monkhouse. The surgeon looked inside then back along the ranks. "Sinners," he said, "the hat's going around again so fill it up. And whoever took my coin, put it back."

When Evans returned, he simply shook his head.

"Still no money?" his co-leader asked.

Leaning close, the quartermaster whispered in the doctor's ear and the two then faced me and the crew.

"Right," Monkhouse said, "who's got the bloody hat?"

When nobody admitted guilt, Monkhouse looked towards me for assistance. I could see that he was floundering so I told him to forget the collection and close the service with some hymns because a brisk nor'easterley was beginning to blow and it would soon be time to set sail.

Monkhouse seemed desperate to make a better impression, so he quickly said, "Mister Evans, would you please lead us in the singing. Let that Welsh baritone of yours fill every nook in this ship. Men, the hymn is

'Guide Me, O Thou Great Jehovah'. On the count of two...one..."

"You would have to pick that one," Evans interrupted. "I don't know it."

The surgeon looked at me sheepishly. "Never mind. How about 'Rock of Ages'?"

Evans shook his head.

"'Jesus Wants Me for A Sunbeam'?"

"Sorry."

In desperation, Monkhouse pleaded, "Do you know anything you can lead us in?"

The chorister waved his finger in the air excitedly and said, "How about temptation?"

Without stopping to consider the effect his actions would have on the rest of the crew, Monkhouse grabbed the quartermaster round the throat and shouted, "If you're being deliberately provocative, then I promise that your rich baritone will soon become a soprano envied by every castrato in Christendom! Now think of something more appropriate and make it quick!"

Evans scratched his head for a second or two then replied, "All I know is a Welsh poem me Sunday School teacher taught me when I was a kid in Swansea."

Producing what appeared to be a relieved smile, the surgeon instructed him to carry on. The quartermaster, suitably chastened, stood to attention, clasped his hairy hands reverently behind his back, filled his great lungs with air and said, "You'll all know this one. I'll give you the first few lines and then you join in. Here goes. The boyo stood on the rolling deck, amid the howling squalls. An icy gust blew up his pants and froze off both his..."

PLOTS, CLOTS and CALAMITY | 123

A gnawing sense of dismay had been stalking my optimism from the moment the service started, and like a lion just released from its cage, I leapt forward and roared, "Boatswain, dismiss the men!"

Most of the hope I'd held about securing the crew's allegiance vanished with their dismissal. With a pounding head, I stood on the quarter-deck and surveyed the horizon. A blue line across a black day. To the west, clouds were building, their distant drizzle floating down like soot-dust. One or two spots of rain fell on my boots, making small, bleached circles in the dark polish. The air seemed to suddenly expand and chill. It was time to go.

"Mr Hicks, have the men stand by the windlass. I want the anchor up as soon as possible. Boatswain, make ready to get under way."

"Aye aye."

With the wind in the mainsail and the hull cresting wave after wave, the ship gathered speed, finally easing to a steady four knots. When I retired at midnight, the day's events kept running through my mind, so I got up and took what Monkhouse called the 'seaman's cure'; three rums in three seconds. The following morning, Mr Orton woke me with a cup of tea. I greeted him with half-opened eyes and asked if his hearing was better.

"It's about six-thirty," he replied.

Remembering, albeit foggily, that another shore excursion had been scheduled, I swallowed the tea in one great gulp and told Orton to send the shore party to the cabin. Five minutes later he came back with a shoe and a pastry, so I simply wrote what I wanted on a piece of paper and gave it to him. Hicks, Pickersgill, Tupia and several marines arrived just as I finished dressing. Mr Banks, recruited so that I could keep a close watch on his activities, appeared several minutes later, leading his whippet. Rather than apologising for his tardiness, he berated the others for being early. I let the incident pass without comment, choosing instead to remind everyone of the excursion's purpose; to survey and chart the terrain north of several islands sighted the previous day. They'd all been lush with tropical forests and ringed by sands as white as any English snow. All the colours of the rainbow could be seen in the feathers of the birds that nested in the trees, and the waters that lapped at the beaches graduated from light green in close to sapphire blue further out. I'd named the largest of these islands 'Great Keppel' after the distinguished English seaman, Admiral Augustus Keppel. A man supposedly gifted in matters of commerce, it was Keppel who observed after he and Sir George Pocock had led a successful expedition against Havana in 1762, 'This place will never be known for anything until the people stop smoking those noxious brown-leaf things.'

Gastro gave us a hearty breakfast of oatmeal and supplied the party with enough victuals to last the day; goat-cheese, oat-cakes, water and a small cask of beer. At nine on the dot, the marines, bearing arms in case of trouble, loaded the supplies into the long-boat and we set off. After an hour's strenuous rowing we arrived, dragged the long-boat up onto the shore, secured it with rope and peg then unloaded the equipment. A rough path, apparently beaten down by the feet of the natives, could be seen winding through the scrub, so we followed it. It extended for a quarter of a mile and stopped at the base of a hill. From the top of the hill, the surrounding countryside was clearly visible, so the theodolite was set up. After an hour's trouble-free surveying in heat that could blister hardwood, I told the men to refresh themselves at a nearby watering-hole. Thankful, they dropped everything and dashed off. Hicks arrived first and stood at the edge of the hole.

"Let's do this properly," he said. "Trousers rolled up? Vests tucked in? Handkerchiefs tied at the corners and on the heads? Good. Come on, let's go! First one in gets a bottle of port!"

Nobody moved, including Hicks.

"Last one in gets a bottle of port?"

A mad rush followed and they all dived in as one, laughing and drinking the crystal water from cupped hands. After a few minutes of mucking about, Banks reminded everyone that he had won the archery contest back in Otaheite and then laid claim to being the best swimmer. Pickersgill protested, wagering a guinea that *he* was. "You can even nominate the stroke, Mr Banks," he challenged.

On watch a short distance away, I could see Banks mulling the matter over. He chose his words carefully. "I'm not a strong over-armer, so would you be happy to watch me dog-paddle twice around the hole in less than thirty seconds?"

The instant Pickersgill nodded his acceptance, Banks picked up his whippet and threw it in. When the dog had completed two circuits, Banks dragged it out, grinned at Pickersgill then said, "Twenty-three seconds it took him to paddle the distance. Let's have the guinea."

In order to mediate on what had been an obvious swindle, I'd left my post and was heading towards the hole. Just as I reached it, a twig snapped and we all spun around.

"It's the Heathen," Private Dunster shouted as several black-skinned warriors bore down on us. To my surprise, I noticed that their leader was the same one who had been kicked in the privates by Gore several days earlier. He must have been following us up the coast, intent on revenge.

"Form two lines," I shouted. "Marines in front, the rest kneeling behind. I want a warning volley above their heads. If that doesn't stop them, shoot to kill."

Three muskets fired simultaneously, and when the smoke cleared, the natives had also. But not for long. They'd been hiding in a nearby thicket, and as the marines prepared to reload, they burst out with wild eyes and terrifying wails, hurling clubs, spears and rocks. Dodging the missiles as best we could, we then regrouped behind the marines as they took aim. I gave the order to fire and Dunster let loose a volley that peppered the chief with enough shot to turn him into a salt-shaker. Screeching louder than the panicked cockatoos that erupted from the tree-tops, the wounded chief dropped to the ground like a sack of grain. At once, his tribesmen threw their remaining weapons aside, hoisted him onto their shoulders and fled into the scrub.

"We routed 'em good and proper," Dunster bellowed as he jumped up and down. Banks, obviously wanting some of the glory, then asked if anyone had seen him take on two of the natives bare-handed.

"No," Pickersgill said.

"You should've," Banks stated.

"We would've if you had've," Dunster declared, putting the botanist's feet of clay back firmly on the ground.

Fearing that our attackers might return in even greater numbers and with stouter determination, I told Dunster to be quiet, reload all the barking irons and keep his eyes open. We then gathered up the surveying equipment and headed back to the long-boat. Our caution was unnecessary because we arrived at the shore untroubled, the natives apparently having left the vicinity after the earlier clash.

There was a sense of relief among the lads as they loaded the boat and prepared to put out. They chatted incessantly, laughed and slapped each other on the back. It was good to see. In the same spirit, and just as the oars were raised, I praised them for meeting their test with courage. The effect was immediate. With a tremendous surge of pride, Dunster and Pickersgill plunged their oars into the water and pulled like they'd never pulled before. The other rowers quickly joined them, and with the golden sheen of twilight glowing on their faces, it wasn't long before the ship loomed up.

It was then that dread seized me. Doing a quick head-count, I realised someone was missing. Tupia.

"Turn about," I ordered.

Although we were only an oar's-length from the *Endeavour*, Hicks immediately grabbed the tiller and swung us about. Then, just as the bow was pointing towards the shore, Tupia's hands emerged from the water and grabbed hold of the port-side rowlock.

"Natives steal me," he spluttered as he dragged himself in. "Wanted me to be new chief. Me run away. Me buggered."

When we finally managed to haul him onto the *Endeavour's* deck, he was in obvious need of medical attention, so I sent for the surgeon. Monkhouse arrived with Mr Gore a few minutes later and carried out a cursory examination by lantern light.

"He's wet and tired," Monkhouse said, "but he'll be right tomorrow. Good night."

Gore immediately blocked the surgeon's path and held the lantern in front of his face. "You've had years of medical learning," the lieutenant fumed, "and that's the best you can come up with? You're a bloody charlatan!"

It was clear that Monkhouse was as drunk as a duke in the House of Lords, so I told Gore to let him be.

"But, Sir," he persisted, "it's rubbish to say that Tupia's only tired. Look at him. He hasn't even got the strength to change his mind."

Monkhouse was wobbling from side to side and breathing heavily into the lantern, so I ordered Gore to take it away in case the fumes ignited and blew us all to pieces. As the light fell, the surgeon's anger rose.

"What would you know about medicine, Gore? You're the sort of intellectual sluggard who thinks a case of cholera improves if it's left in the cellar for a year before decanting."

Just then, a swell rolled under the ship and we listed to port. A second later, a loud belch rumbled from Monkhouse and he listed to starboard. With as much dignity as he could muster, he jabbed his finger into

Gore's chest and threatened to report his insolence to the Admiralty when we got home. He then stumbled his way along the deck, looking for the hatch. His feet found it, but his head insisted on going down first.

It was getting frosty so I ordered Dunster and Pickersgill to carry Tupia to his hammock and cover him with blankets. Any deterioration or improvement in his condition was to be reported to me immediately. Stuffing my hands deeply into my coat pockets, I then went below to my cabin, leaving Gore to appoint the watch.

Mr Orton had been considerate enough to place a cup of steaming coffee on my desk. I sipped it with gratitude. The log needed to be filled in, and as I picked up my quill, my mind drifted to the quarrel between Gore and Monkhouse. Had I not been present, it may well have turned violent. The prospect was intolerable. This distaste for violence had resulted from my period as master aboard the *Northumberland* at the end of the war against the French in North America. When Quebec capitulated in 1760, there was little for our sailors to do, and the smallest infraction often brought dire results; yardarm hangings, lengthy imprisonment and the ever present lash. One sailor has stayed in my mind all these years; Edward Lovely. In the space of five months he received more than 600 strokes. Brutality disguised as justice administered by bullies. While I condoned the use of the lash while commanding the *Endeavour*, no-one could ever accuse me of overstepping the mark. Banks may have been looking for reasons to topple me, but he wouldn't find any in the punishment book.

The sudden thought of Banks brought with it the need for fresh air, so I leaned back in my chair, reached up and opened the window. A gust rushed in and rustled through the log's pages. Outside, the stars clustered and winked like fire-flies. About ten miles to the west, the hump that was *Cape Townshend* rose from the water like some huge, dark whale. I was about to dip the nib into the ink-well when I heard a clear voice from the deck above.

"She's a bit nippy." It was Midshipman Jonathan Monkhouse, the surgeon's younger brother. A second voice, Lieutenant Gore's, was equally distinct.

"Yes, Midshipman. Anything to report?"

"No, Sir."

"You're cold?"

"Yes, Sir."

"No coat?"

"Correct."

"I'll have one sent up."

"Thank you."

Gore's tone then became less formal. "Jonathan, I'm curious about something. Is your brother vindictive?"

"What's that mean?"

"Does he hold grudges?"

"No. Given the amount he drinks, it's a miracle he can hold a glass."

"So if he threatened to report someone, say an officer, he wouldn't actually do it?"

"Are you the officer?"

"Yes."

"Forget it. He only blusters like that when he's pissed."

Gore's voiced dropped as the wind picked up. "Will he ever stop drinking?"

"Yep. The minute he stops breathing."

"So you think I'm safe?"

"Only if you don't get sick."

"Do you let him treat you?"

"Never. William couldn't recognise a temperature in a furnace."

"I'm glad we've had this talk, Jonathan. I feel much more relaxed."

"Don't mention it."

"Trust me, I won't. Goodnight, Midshipman."

It was a disturbing conversation for two reasons. First, it showed Gore to be susceptible to intimidation, a weakness unacceptable in officers. Second, it focused clearly on the major problem blighting the voyage so far; if brothers had no respect for each other, heaven help the rest of the crew.

At close to 4 a.m., and being unable to sleep, I decided that Hicks should suffer likewise, so I dressed and went to his cabin. He was out like a snuffed candle. I shook him awake violently and told him we were going to inspect the ship. "But I'm half-asleep," he whined.

"As long as it's the half that talks, I don't mind."

Five minutes later, with Hicks holding the lantern, we made our way through the hushed ship to the storage vessels in the hold. Everything seemed in order, with no water evident in the coal for the galley, the carpenters' timber and the various casks and sacks. Further forward was the magazine. As we approached it, the sentry on duty, Private Wilshire, clicked his heels to attention and said, "Halt! Who goes there?"

Hicks gave our names and Wilshire told us to step forward. We did as ordered. When we were formally recognised, I asked the sentry if everything was ship-shape. He nodded, then added as an after-thought, "Why is everyone up so early?"

Hicks asked what he meant and Wilshire said that Joseph Banks and Charles Green were in the magazine checking on something.

I immediately told them both to be quiet, waved Wilshire away, put out the lantern then tip-toed to the door. Hicks followed. From inside, I could hear muffled voices. My hand slowly turned the latch and a fissure appeared, large enough for us to have a partial view without betraying our presence. Joseph was standing next to one of the powder kegs, discussing the contents of a piece of paper with Green.

"Do you think it'll work, Charles?"

The observer's face was a cowardly yellow in the light of the covered lantern. He sounded hesitant. "I don't know and I'm not sure I want to get involved. What happens to me if I help and you fail?"

"I won't. Everything's down on paper."

To prove his point, he moved the lantern close to the paper and indicated a passage. "See how carefully I've detailed the central figure's failings. He's a jumped-up, working-class tyrant who's made it to captain by ingratiating himself with his betters."

Green's words were cautionary rather than confirming. "Yes, but you're taking on something that's outside your experience. No matter how well you've planned it, the unexpected can occur."

"That's why I've approached you. Up till now I've kept it hush-hush but I need someone else to check to see if I've missed anything. Dot all the Ts, cross all the Is, etcetera."

His fellow conspirator made a feeble attempt to lesson the tension. "I'll miss everything if my eyes are crossed. But seriously, I'm nervous. Why don't you talk to Hicks? He knows the way things are done in the navy."

"True," Banks conceded, "but Hicks has a big mouth. One word to him and my plot would be common knowledge within ten minutes. Any number of people could then claim to have thought of it and I'd receive no acknowledgement or praise."

Suddenly the lantern flickered and a dark, conspiratorial silence filled the magazine. Green's silhouette shuffled slightly within the cramped quarters, his fingers pushing through his hair. "I need more time to think about it."

"Okay, but don't tell anyone about this. When the time's right, they'll all know."

Quietly closing the door, I grabbed Hicks' arm. We then stepped carefully around the stores and, in complete darkness, made our way back to my cabin. When the door was safely locked behind us, I positioned a chair at the front of my desk for the lieutenant. After he'd slumped into it, I asked for his thoughts about what had just occurred.

Zachariah crossed his legs, clasped his hands behind his head and replied, "I don't like to say this, but I reckon he's trying to gain support for a plot against you."

As my fingers drummed a concerned tattoo on the top of the desk, my eyes stayed fixed on Zachariah. I then poured us both a rum and confirmed his suspicions. Hicks uncrossed his legs, gulped down his measure and asked why I hadn't confronted the turncoats. I rose from my chair and sat on the edge of the desk. "How could I? There was no direct mention of mutiny, no overt threat. Just a general discussion of me and my apparent shortcomings."

Hicks took my point and nodded his agreement. I then walked over to the window and gazed out. The shell of the sun was just appearing above the horizon; a new day was hatching. I tugged at the stubble on my chin, looked back at Zachariah and stated the facts. "Had we burst into the magazine and accused Banks, we would've been on very shaky ground. He'd have denied any so-called plot and it would simply be my word against his, if and when charges are brought. And considering his highly-placed friends, you can bet he'd walk out of the room a free man and I'd be left a laughing-stock with egg on my face."

"Probably only the shells, given the likelihood that Lord Sandwich would be presiding over the hearing."

I didn't appreciate the flippant remark, or the frequent liberties the lieutenant was taking with the rum, so I snatched the bottle away and told him to be serious. After a couple of minutes' silence, an idea took hold. We had to look for an opportunity to establish Banks' guilt that was weighted more in my favour. Solid evidence from an impeccable character was needed. Hicks thought the plan was sound and suggested Robert Molyneux.

"Impeccable, not impeachable. No, I need someone else. Reach around the desk, get the muster-roll from the drawer and read out the names." The early morning light now made the lantern redundant, so Hicks pushed it aside and placed the roll in the middle of the desk. His voice was matter-of-fact.

"Dozey, John."

"Keep going."

"Pickersgill, Richard."

"Pick another."

"Matthews, Thomas."

"Go on."

"Orton, Charles."

"He's deaf. Next."

"Sutherland, Forby."

"He's dead. Next."

"Monkhouse, William."

"He isn't, unfortunately. Next."

"Evans, Samuel. He's good in a crisis."

"No, he's good *for* a crisis. Next."

There was a pause as Hicks cast his eyes down the remainder of the list. His finger went back up a little way. "What about Peckover?"

"Peckover! Good grief! Can't you just hear him? 'Beggin' the Cap'n's pardon, but would a wolf in ship's clothin' be the same as mutiny dressed as lamb?' I'd rather have Black Beard."

Again Hicks' finger shifted up and down. "Beard, Black? Sorry, he's not listed."

"That's only because he doesn't want to get himself a bad name through association. Who's next?"

"We're running out of candidates, apart from Mr Gore."

"Let's *keep* him apart."

"That leaves the sailmaker, John Ravenhill."

It was as if rock had struck rock and sparked. Why hadn't I thought of old 'Sails' in the first place? He'd been at sea for most of his seventy years, and I'd never heard a bad word against him. His testimony would never be doubted. Having determined that Ravenhill was the man for the job, I told Hicks to send him to me after breakfast. I also reminded the lieutenant of the need for secrecy. A word in the wrong ear, any ear for that matter, could be disastrous.

At precisely 9 a.m., the old sailmaker knocked on the door and announced himself. When he entered, he looked about the cabin and said, "Very nice. Lots of books, a desk, a couple of soft chairs. The Admiralty sure looks after its shining lights, and rightly so. Yours is a mighty tough job."

Pointing to one of the chairs he'd been admiring, I asked him to sit. He smiled, scratched his wiry, grey beard then settled his bony frame into the leather. In the light, the years of experience were deeply etched in the lines of his brown, weather-beaten face.

I asked if he'd like a mug of coffee. He said he'd prefer a neat rum. I said I'd prefer if he didn't. He then suggested a compromise; a mug of rum with a dash of coffee. I nodded. He winked. We were off to a promising start.

"John," I began, pulling my chair up next to his, "I can tell you're not one for messing about, so I'll get straight to the point. I need your help." His mouth was wide open as I told him of the events surrounding Banks' plan for mutiny.

"Skipper," he whispered after hearing the tale, "boy and man I've been around ships, hearing stories that'd make stiffs sit up, but this is the worst. Banks, of all people! And Charles Green! I know he's an astronomer of high repute because Mr Gore told me that he'd had a haemorrhoid named after him."

"I think you'll find that it was an asteroid, John," I corrected, "but he's a pain in the arse so you might be right."

Ravenhill added a dash more rum to his coffee and touched my forearm in a fatherly fashion. "James, are you sure about all this? Banks has got some powerful friends. You mess with him without evidence and you could find yourself on some old scow dragging dead'ns from the Thames for the rest of your life."

The sailmaker stood up and cracked the knuckles of his fingers, one by one. He then twisted his wrists, and they too cracked. As he was about to manipulate his elbows, I said, "Stop that and sit down. I need your help to get the evidence."

Ravenhill sat forward, his wrinkled hands firmly clutching his knees. "I'm listening."

My throat was dry so I took a sip of coffee. Old 'Sails' swallowed his in one gulp then held out his cup for more. I poured until it was just about full, added a small measure of coffee and said, "For the next twelve hours I want you to follow Mr Banks and meticulously note every move he makes. If he speaks to someone, write down that person's name. If you're close enough to hear the conversation, record every word of it. When I finally bring charges against the perfidious popinjay, I want a cartload of irrefutable evidence. With it, you'll be the man who stands next to me and points the accusing finger."

"There's only one problem," Ravenhill said, looking at his hand. I glanced down. His disjointed finger was pointing directly at me.

"Permission to put it back into place?"

"Granted."

When I heard the crack, I looked again. This time the finger was pointing straight at him.

"Permission to try again?"

"Refused. Put it in your pocket."

"But, Skipper, I can't go around like that. Pickersgill will think I'm pleased to see him."

"No-one will see you. You'll be keeping yourself well hidden."

A surge of confidence infused the sailmaker and his chest rose. "I'll give it a go. With the Almighty at the tiller and us two at the rowlocks, I reckon we can do it."

His Christian outlook surprised me as no-one else on board apparently shared it, judging by the recent service. It was also refreshingly basic, because the last theological discussion I'd had with one of the crew had reflected an appalling lack of understanding. It occurred in Otaheite when Gathrey asked if the Book of Psalms gave instructions on how to shake coconuts loose without being hit on the noggin.

"Next time we have a service," I said as Ravenhill stood to leave, "I'll let you conduct it."

"When will that be?"

"I'll need to look at the barometer."

"Why?"

"Because it'll indicate when Hell's frozen over. Let me have your report as soon as possible and may the Lord go with you."

Old 'Sails' opened the door then looked back. "I know He will, but on the off chance He forgets or oversleeps, how about an armed escort as well?"

As reassurance, I reminded Ravenhill that Banks was only interested in getting rid of me. Unconvinced, he frowned slightly and was about to leave when I called him back.

"There's something else you want me to do, Skip?"

"Yes. Take the bottle of rum out of your breeches and put it back on the desk."

In the silence that followed his departure, the ship's timbers creaked their age, and from the wall clock, the seconds ticked louder and louder, gathering till they finally burst against my eardrums like a volley from an ever-echoing musket.

The remainder of the day was spent in solitary charting, and at 9 p.m., a quiet yet insistent rapping on the door caused me to put the pencil down. I asked who it was. The reply was a muffled whisper. "Ravenhill. I've got that thing you wanted."

When I opened the door, the trembling sailmaker glanced right and left over his shoulders then scurried in. From his jacket, he took several sheets of crumpled paper and handed them to me. Being anxious to study his work, I took the sheets nearer the desk and asked if he'd met with any trouble. Ravenhill walked stiffly over and stood next to me, wheezing like a set of untuned bag-pipes. "Nothing I couldn't handle," he said proudly.

"I stuck with Mr Banks all day and every nasty, back-stabbing move he made is there. Any chance of one of those special coffees?"

I patted him on the back, an experience similar to stroking an emaciated cat, and told him to help himself.

"Thanks," he said, emptying the dregs of my cup into the saucer, "but I'll leave the coffee out, otherwise I'll be awake all night."

With the report firmly in my grip, I moved closer to the lantern. "If this contains the evidence I'm anticipating, then we'll both sleep like logs."

The flame flickered slightly as I settled the papers next to it. A hurried, though legible, hand had been at work and the notes were brief but to the point.

'Report on activities of one J. Banks arising from certain alligations. The alligator is one J. Cook.
6.07 a.m. Suspect joined officers and other gentlemen in mess for the breaking of fast.
6.23 a.m. Suspect joined officers and other gentlemen on poop-deck for the breaking of wind. Suspect spoke to Mr Hicks. Said 'I wish Gastro would serve something other than sour kraut'.
6.24 a.m. Suspect went below and brought up whippet. Tied it to mizzen-mast.
6.25 a.m. Suspect went below and brought up sour kraut. Returned to quarter-deck. Untied dog, waved stick in its face and then threw it overboard.
6.26 a.m. Mr Hicks said to suspect 'Why did you throw your dog overboard?' The two exchanged words. Suspect said 'You're as bright as a total eclipse of the sun'. Mr

Hicks said 'Engage the services of a covent garden nun' or something along similar lines.

7.02 a.m. Dog paddled back to ship and suspect walked it around quarter-deck. Took dog back to hold.

7.04 a.m. Suspect escorted back to quarter-deck by boatswain. Boatswain waved stick in suspect's face. Boatswain said 'Scrape that dog shit off your shoe with this and then chuck it in the water!' Suspect followed boatswain's orders.

7.05 a.m. Boatswain said to suspect 'Why did you throw your shoe in the water?' Both men exchanged words. Suspect said 'I hate you'. Boatswain said 'The feeling's mutual'. Suspect said 'That means we both hate you.' Suspect laughed. Boatswain didn't.

7.07 a.m. Suspect approached me. Said 'Why are you hiding behind the fore-mast and why have you been staring at me for the past hour?'

7.07 and a bit a.m. I said 'Who, me?'

7.07 and a bit more a.m. Suspect said 'Yes, you.'

7.07 just going on 08 a.m. I said 'I just got here.'

7.08 on the dot a.m. Suspect said 'You're a betwattled old prick who wouldn't know a cross-stitch from a camel's arse!' Suspect got cranky look on face.

7.08 etc a.m. Suspect raised fist.

7.08 etc etc my hand is sore from all this writing a.m. I ran away and hid in hold.

3.26 p.m. Came back to quarter-deck. Suspect was walking along deck wearing boatswain's shitless shoes. Suspect saw me and chased me down to hold. Locked me in.

3.26 and a bit p.m. Received bite on ankle from field-mouse.

8.43 p.m. Boatswain let me out of hold. I said "Have you seen Mr Banks?' Boatswain said 'He's in his cabin. Have you seen anyone wearing my fuckin' shoes?'
8.43 and a bit p.m. I said 'You wear special shoes when you're on the bonk?'
8.44 p.m. Boatswain chased me back to hold and locked me in.
8.59 p.m. Escaped from hold when Mr Orton and two sailors snuck in for game of 7-card poker.
9.00 p.m. Took report back to Captain Cook.'

"You wasted twelve hours compiling *this*?" I asked.

Ravenhill was uncorking another rum bottle. "No, fourteen," he mumbled, his eyes reddening.

My head was pounding. "Do you really expect that a specially-convened hearing would consider this report as admissible evidence? Ravenhill, it's evidence of only two things; your incompetence and my poor judgement in employing you. It's a cart-load, all right, but not of evidence. I'm only sorry that we don't have a garden on board that needs fertilising! Now get out of my sight before I do something I might regret. And if you breathe a word of this to anyone, *you'll* be the one on the scow dragging bloaters from the Thames."

To his credit, 'Sails' meekly apologised, drew himself up next to my ear and whispered.

"No," I bellowed, "you *can't* have another special coffee. Now fuck off!"

It had been a long and tiring day, so after Ravenhill's rickety frame rattled into the corridor, I put out the lantern, walked slowly over to my bunk, removed my uniform and stretched out. In the chrysalis of the cabin, all was cool and butterfly quiet. The light from the moon washed against the window and the frame cast a criss-cross shadow on the far wall. Apart from the slap of the water against the bow as the ship moved steadily forward, and the muffle of voices from the men on watch, there were no other noises. It felt good to be off my feet, and sleep, albeit light, came almost at once. Regrettably, the respite was short-lived because there was another knock at the door the second my eyes closed.

"Whoever it is, go away. Mr Gore is the officer on watch. See him." No more than ten seconds passed before the tapping resumed.

"If that's you, Ravenhill, look out!"

"It ain't 'Sails', Cap'n, it's me, Gastro."

The relaxation that I had momentarily enjoyed quickly turned to tension. I tried to keep my eyes closed but it was impossible, so I asked him what he wanted.

"I've got somethin' for you. Can I come in?"

"If you must," I replied curtly. "I suppose the sooner you do the sooner I'll be rid of you."

Like a footman entering his master's honeymoon suite just after the snuffing of the candle, the cook stepped inside. "Sorry for the disturbance," he whispered as he tiptoed towards the bunk, "but I noticed you weren't at mess tonight so I've taken the liberty of bringin' your food to you."

His kindness immediately placated my coldness. I fumbled for the lantern, lit it then thanked him for his thoughtfulness. Now Thompson had a reputation for being rather eccentric but his appearance on this occasion placed him at the very top of England's strangest. As he stepped into the arc of light around the bunk, I saw with wall-clawing disbelief that he was wearing a woollen head-dress that covered his neck and the sides of his face. If I hadn't heard about his ardency in Otaheite, I may have thought that he'd taken final vows.

"Thompson, have you gone completely insane? Why are you wearing that nun's garment?"

"Because it keeps my head warm these chilly nights. Care to try it on?"

"No! Just show me what's on the tray."

Thompson placed it on the table beside the bunk and said, "You'll like it. Master Molyneux took a hunting party ashore today and they came back with a wild pig. I've made it into something special."

"I don't want to hear a single crewman's name. Just tell me what you've brought."

"Your favourite. A delicious pork sausage."

By now the smell had reached my nose, bringing with it a degree of comfort. "Gastro, this is the only good thing to have come out of this day. It's been two years since I've tasted a sausage. Elizabeth prepared one the night before the ship left England. I'm grateful for both the treat and the memory it inspires."

Thompson handed me a knife and fork. "You deserve it because you've had a lot to put up with lately. Are you sure you won't try on my head warmer?"

All I wanted was a quiet meal, so I said emphatically, "No, just go and let me eat my sausage in peace."

And so ended the month of May, not with a wimple but a banger.

Washed Up
June 1770

During the first week of June, as the *Endeavour* continued her steady, northern course, much of our time was spent navigating through the islands, capes and bays that featured in this area of the coastline. It was an exercise fraught with danger. Constant soundings were necessary because one minute saw the water deep enough to proceed with safety, the next saw it barely covering a reef. In order to assist the helmsman in steering the least dangerous course, a lookout was permanently stationed, his loud and urgent calls of 'port' or 'starboard' never allowing us to relax.

As well as supervising the navigation, I was also responsible for charting. It was a hectic time, and I became so preoccupied with performing my duties and ensuring the men's safety that I neglected the state of my own health. This lapse was to have dire consequences, the most dreadful being the *Endeavour's* running aground.

The train of events which eventually culminated in this catastrophe began on Friday the 8th. Heavy rain the previous night had abated by the time the sun rose, and high across the port-side hills arched a glorious rainbow. Later, at around noon, when we were in the Latitude 17°59′South and about two leagues from shore, the officer on watch, John Gore, reported the sighting of two significant points of land, so I left my cabin and went atop. A fresh breeze pushed at my face as I emerged through the hatch and the first feature immediately came into view. It was of moderate height, and because of its shape, I called it *Point Hillock*. A short distance from it, another headland jutted into the sea, and at its base, waves pounded themselves into sheets of spray and white foam. To this feature I gave the name *Iron Head*, in recognition of Gore's involvement in its sighting. Between *Point Hillock* and *Iron Head*, the shore formed a large bay, with some of the greenest water ever seen lapping onto the whitest sand imaginable. Gore cast his eyes around the fertile area then proposed that it be called *Halifax Bay* after George Montagu Dunk, the 2nd Earl of Halifax. He had been president of the Board of Trade for almost twelve years, and the lieutenant said, without any attempt at disguise, that the minor honour could rebound favourably on him if he ever left the navy and went into commerce. Annoyed by his opportunism, I pointed out that he was displaying the sort of attitude commonly seen in Banks.

"Maybe so," he said, squaring his hat, "but who's the wealthy landowner with powerful friends and who's the debt-ridden 3rd lieutenant with no prospects?"

His words had sinister implications and I felt that Banks might have gained a cohort. Unwilling to give him further reason to betray me, I agreed with his name for the bay and went below. As I opened the cabin door, I sensed his presence lingering behind me like some odour from Nottingham's main sewer, the River Leen.

"I'm busy," I said, turning to face him.

Noticing my displeasure, he stepped back a discreet distance and replied, "Captain, about Mr Hicks. As you've probably heard…"

I was in no mood to suffer any more grizzles, so I put my hand up, told him to solve the matter himself then closed the door in his face. After recording the bay's name in the log and on the chart, there was further work to be done, external to the ship, so I sent for Mr Hicks and instructed him to lower the yawl. Fresh supplies were needed urgently, and here was an area worth investigating. Hicks was prompt in following the order, and with Carpenter Satterley and Able Seaman Antonio Ponto manning the oars, the four of us struck out for the shore. A sizeable chop and an enervating heat made the job of rowing all the more taxing.

Upon arrival, we dragged the yawl up onto the grass behind the beach, caught our breaths then looked around for any natives who might have been lurking in the encircling trees. There appeared to be none, but I did notice the small, round droppings of the marsupial that we had often seen on previous excursions. In many ways these brown, long-tailed creatures were unique, bearing their young in pouches and leaping about with tremendous vitality.

"These look like a 'roo's," I said, pointing to the droppings.

The lieutenant prodded at the deposits with the end of his boot and said, somewhat cryptically, "No, they're genuine."

After twenty seconds of bewildered thought the light finally dawned. "Lieutenant, I didn't mean a 'ruse' as in 'trick'. I meant a kangaroo's been here."

Relishing Hicks' misunderstanding, Ponto and Satterley looked at each other and sniggered. I could see that Hicks was getting hot under the collar, physically as well as in attitude, so to avoid the inevitable intersecting of crossed words, I instructed the men to separate and reconnoitre.

"Mr Hicks, you go north, Satterley, you go south, I'll go west and Ponto, you stay and guard the yawl. We'll meet back here in two hours."

As the men headed in their respective directions, another thought occurred to me, so I called them back and said, "If you encounter any belligerent natives, try to win them over with trinkets. If that fails, remember to fire a warning shot above their heads. If they still want to fight after you've taken all necessary steps to preserve life, then you have my permission to take more drastic action."

"You mean run like hell," Satterley said as he lumbered off with a musket over each shoulder.

My survey through the low-lying scrub and dunes produced little in terms of provisions, there being nothing to the west apart from a few coconuts. So after the time specified, I returned to the beach to find Hicks and Satterley sitting on the sand. They were empty-handed.

"No water, no food, nothin'," the carpenter said, shaking his head.

His lack of fresh supplies was disappointing, but an even greater cause for concern was the fact that his muskets were missing. As I slumped down beside him, I asked for an explanation.

"I gave 'em to some natives I bumped into a little ways in."

Hicks was disbelieving. Before I could stop him, he grabbed Satterley's shoulders, shook for all he was worth and demanded to know the reason. As if totally innocent, the carpenter held out his calloused hands and replied, "I was followin' the cap'n's orders. He told us to be friendly so I presented 'em as gifts."

Like a cat on a rat, Zachariah pinned the struggling Satterley to the sand and hissed, "Why didn't you give them something less dangerous, say some baubles?"

"Left 'em on board."

"Bangles?"

"Lost 'em overboard."

"Bright shiny beads?"

"Dumped 'em out of me pocket because they kept bangin' against me jing-jingalingas."

My voice was a thunder-clap. "Didn't you stop to consider that the heathens could charge down here and use those very same muskets against us?"

The carpenter's voice was an echo of mine. "I didn't stop to consider anythin'. I was too busy runnin' like hell! Straight up, it was the worst hour of me life!"

Not to be outdone, Lieutenant Hicks shoved his face directly in front of Satterley's and shouted, "But you just told me you'd only gone fifty yards inland before you met the savages. An hour to run back fifty yards? Impossible!"

At this stage, the only impossibility seemed to be louder shouting, but Satterley quickly proved that wrong. Thumping his knee with his knuckles and filling his lungs, he exploded indignantly, "Let's see *you* try light-heelin' it with a wooden leg! Run, clunk, unplug it, run, clunk, unplug it again! Got the picture?"

The picture was indeed gloomy, made even bleaker by the fact that the rainbow had long since vanished. With twilight now approaching, I thought it best that we return to the ship, so I stood to issue the order. As I was about to speak, the fever that had gripped me in

April again took hold and I stumbled. Hicks noticed my unsteadiness and asked if I was all right.

"No," I said, my head spinning, "so just give me a minute to compose myself." The shadows from the trees lay themselves out along the width of the beach, and the air was sharp and chilled.

An hour later the yawl finally pulled in alongside the *Endeavour*, and Hicks and I climbed up the rope ladder leading to the main deck. Fatigued and wobbly, I paused to gather my breath then told the lieutenant that if I was forced to my bed, he would be in charge till I recovered. As I recall, he looked down at my feet and mumbled something about my boots being hard to fill. Then he stared at my head, said that my hat looked about the right size and asked if he could try it on. Although feeling poorly, I was still able to voice a definite 'no'. A shawl of disappointment hung over Zachariah's shoulders, but it was soon replaced by the mantle of a more sinister apprehension.

"Captain," he said as he gazed around the deck, "do you notice anything strange?"

Even in my febrile state I had, and there was good reason for our concern. The deck should have been busy with several men on evening watch, but there was none. Not a single soul. The only sound came from the night breeze as it pressured and moaned about the slack rigging, and the only detectable movement was the placid rocking of our ship as she lay at anchor. All around her was a lightless sky and ghosts of past dishonours.

"Mr Hicks," I whispered, "make a search below to see if there's anyone there."

Quickly stepping forward, Satterley pushed gently at the lieutenant's chest and said, "No. You stay here and look after the cap'n. Ponto and me'll go." Two minutes later they were back. Satterley's eyes were narrow in the dimness. "Quiet as a tomb and just as cold. There ain't nobody down there. And it's pitch bloody black."

Ponto agreed with a nod of his idea pot and added, "And it's bloody scary as well."

There was only one conclusion to be drawn and I instantly jumped to it. Leading Hicks away from the others so as not to be heard, I whispered, "This is Banks' doing. He's convinced the men that I'm a tyrant and they've all deserted. My friend, there are only four of us on this ship."

Hicks cast a quick glance back over his shoulder and said gravely, "*Were* only four. Satterley and his gutless mate have gone as well."

The situation was becoming blacker by the minute. In an attempt to banish the deleterious effects of the fever, I shook my head and slapped my cheeks lightly. It seemed to work. As I regained some sense of determination, I looked at the lieutenant to gauge his state of mind. His ashen face betrayed his concern. I would have none of it, not on my ship, and certainly not at this critical time. Standing erect, I reminded him that he was an officer in His Majesty's service. The bolster had the desired effect. Hicks straightened himself up beside the wheel and asked what I had in mind. By way of reassurance, I calmly said that we were going below to plan a course of action and that given the circumstances, two heads were better than one.

"They're not if they're on the sharp end of a friggin' pike," Hicks mumbled as he followed me down the companionway.

As soon as we reached the bottom step and peered blindly into the darkness of what I took to be the lower deck, the full impact of our altered state struck. Instead of the voices that usually rang loud against the polished brass and timbers, and the hurried activity of almost one hundred men, there was now only an uncanny, coal-black silence lurking. Under ordinary circumstances I would have rejoiced at the changes but these were extraordinary circumstances and the contrast was as welcome as a nightmare in a nursery.

The door to my cabin was only a short distance away, and with Hicks' hand firmly clutching my collar and his icy breath chilling my neck, I stumbled into the portentous gloom. Then, just as my heel came down upon the unseen board, a deafening shout shredded the silence.

"SUR-FUCKIN'-PRISE!"

At once, a dozen flames erupted brilliantly, and there, packed either along the length of the deck or emerging from cabins, hold or galley, was the crew, each man wearing the biggest smile imaginable. And hanging from a stretched rope across two outer beams was a sign that read; **'HAPPeE BirFDaY MR HIcKs'.**

As I grappled with my fevered thoughts, the truth of what was happening slowly filtered in, and a few seconds later I laughed with pure relief. The feeling was contagious, and Hicks was almost doubled over beside me.

Able Seaman Ponto pushed his way forward. "We had you goin', eh, Cap'n?" he said, handing me a glass of beer.

I sipped at the warm brew, nodded then asked him who had arranged the celebration. Peering through the smoke from lanterns and tobacco-filled pipes, the seaman eventually caught sight of the person responsible and pointed.

"I see. Tell Mr Gore to come here," I said.

On receiving the summons, Gore weaved his way through the throng and crushed up against me. Not wanting to deflate the light-hearted mood, I quietly asked him why he had organised the festivities without first seeking my permission.

"I tried to this morning," he said, "but you told me to work it out myself, remember?"

He was right, so I let the matter drop with the words, "Carry on, but let's keep it short. There's work to be done tomorrow."

Gore smiled, clapped his hands then shouted, "Three cheers for the captain! Hip hip…"

"Hooray!"

"Hip hip…"

"Hooray!"

"Hip hip…"

"Hooray!"

As the final cheer died away, Mr Gathrey threw up his arms and bellowed, "Let's hear it for Mr Hicks. Come on, just like we practised. Ready? After two. One, two… hooray for Zachy, hooray at last, hooray for Zachy, he's a gunner's arsenal!"

When the din dropped, the boatswain looked at Charles Orton standing unsteadily by the beer barrel and loudly chastised him. "Hey, Orton, why didn't you cheer?"

"Get your own beer, dung-drawers," my clerk slurred as he refilled his glass.

Hicks, who by this stage had embraced not only the spirit of the occasion but also every man attending it, finally found his way back to me and gushed, "Isn't life rich? Ten minutes ago I thought my time had come and yet here I am now with more friends than Mr Banks. I'm so happy I feel like running around the deck naked."

On hearing Zachariah's words, Peckover spun around and said, "Beggin' the Lieutenant's pardon, but you be a mighty poor runner so why expose your shortcomin's to everyone?"

A sudden surge of anger engulfed me and I pushed Peckover away. Hicks, misjudging the cause, explained that the seaman hadn't realised that his words could have been construed as a ribald insult.

"I realise that," I said. "It wasn't *his* comment, it was something you just mentioned."

"Me?"

"Yes, you."

"What?"

"Not what, *who*."

"Who?"

"Banks, but forget it. Enjoy your party and tell Mr Gore to meet me on the quarter-deck in two minutes."

Within the confined space, the heat, smoke and my fever were combining with potent effect, so I bustled to the hatch's steps and climbed up. Immediately, the fresh air soothed my eyes. From a distance of almost four miles and charged against the blackness of the night, the orange glow of several fires could be seen along the shore. Behind them, the hills were small, indistinct humps.

"I'm here," Gore said quietly.

I turned around, my anger still simmering, and asked why I hadn't seen Banks at the party.

"I invited him personally," Gore insisted as he leaned against the rail, "but he said he had more important matters to take care of."

"Where is he?"

"In his cabin with Charles Green."

"Any idea what they're up to?"

"Not exactly, but it's my guess it's got something to do with those notes I found back in April; the ones that outlined his intention to get rid of you."

I didn't need to have his plan blurted out for the men on watch to hear, so I told Gore to button his lip and go below to announce that the party would soon end. I remained atop for a few more minutes, mulling over the botanist's snub. While joining in with the common class was obviously not an activity he favoured, signing up others for an uncommon crime was. It was now apparent that Green had been won over. As I stepped down through the hatch, the thought of who would be next to scribble his name, or more likely his X, came up. On reaching the party, I looked around at all the faces. Which one betrayed sinister potential? Whose bright smile could turn dark, given the wrong sort of encouragement? The possibilities were as numerous as the persons, and rather than dwell on the matter, I decided to call a halt to the merriment.

"It's almost midnight," I announced, "and I'm not feeling as well as I should. Start cleaning this mess up because I want you all in your hammocks within thirty minutes."

Stepping forward, Quartermaster Evans thanked me for permitting the party then asked if Mr Hicks could bring it to a close with a speech. The lieutenant, obviously relishing another opportunity to grab centre stage, cleared a circle in the middle of the deck and said, "My pleasure. Captain Cook, Dr Solander, Mr Gore, gentlemen, able seamen, Tupia and marines. I'm overwhelmed by your regard and completely lost for words."

"Good," interrupted Solander, unsteady from too much grog, "now I can go to bed."

I was about to issue the order when Master Molyneux waved his arms like an orchestra conductor and shouted, "There's one final thing. Everybody, after me on the count of four; one, two, four... why was Zach born so beautiful, why was he born so smart, he's not a bag of wind like some, just a clever little fart!" It was a rollicking send-off, loud and full as the singers but flat as the beer.

"Thirty minutes," I repeated, and the cleaning up began. When the floor was finally spotless, the men slung their hammocks and flopped in. After only a few minutes, snoring echoed along the deck. Although loud, it was somehow reassuring, and I tip-toed into my cabin with a sense of relief.

It didn't last long, for as soon as I settled into bed, the fever hit me like a ton of shot and my forehead nearly exploded. On and off I slept, through hours filled with fearful images and voices drifting in and out. When I finally came round, a blurred figure was standing beside my bunk, sponging my brow. He asked how I was feeling. My eyes gradually refocused as I looked up. "Much better, now that the fever's lifted."

The surgeon smiled, drew back the curtain and opened the window. At once, moonglow and a cooling northerly filled the cabin, banishing the staleness of the past hours. Still relatively weak, I eased back the perspiration-soaked blanket and tried to sit up. Monkhouse placed his hands behind my back and told me to be less hasty. My spinning head proved he was right. After he'd propped me up, I asked what time it was. He lengthened the wick of the lantern and the room became familiar as the light spread out.

"It's about six p.m.," he whispered.

"And the day?"

"Sunday the 11th."

I ran my fingers over my chin, scratching at the greying bristles. The 11th. That meant I'd been asleep for three days. With the strain on my arms, I eased myself up a little higher and asked who'd been in charge.

"Mr Hicks," Monkhouse said in a hostile tone.

My body went limp and I slumped back. "And the ship's still in one piece?"

"Yes, but there's been a bit of strife."

The thought of having to listen to an endless litany of woe without sustenance was too much to bear, so I told Monkhouse to bring a bowl of soup and some bread to the cabin. He was to come back with Hicks after I'd eaten. An hour later, the two men stood at the end of the bed. I didn't have the energy to waste words, so I kept my instructions brief.

"I want written reports from both of you concerning what's happened during the past three days. If I'm asleep when you've finished, wake me. Now go and do it."

The next thing I felt was Monkhouse's hand prodding at my shoulder. I opened my eyes and saw Hicks with him. Their reports were on my pillow. I asked Hicks the time and he said that it was close to 9.15 p.m.. "Go to bed," I said. "I want to read these in peace."

Hicks' was the first report studied. The most detailed feature of it was the heading;

'OFFICIAL WRITTEN DECLARATION
A DESCRIPTION OF ACTIVITIES ABOARD H.M.S. ENDEAVOUR
DURING THE MONTH OF JUNE
IN THE YEAR 1770
PREPARED BY 2ND LT. ZACHARIAH HICKS, ACTING CAPTAIN
PERUSAL BY UNAUTHORISED PERSONNEL STRICTLY FORBIDDEN
Friday 9th June, 1770
Light airs at S.E. Three men sick. Lowered anchors. Had men isolated in tent on one of the Frankland Isles. Men treated by Surgeon Monkhouse. All recovered happily. Ship lay at anchor for 24 hours. Peace prevailed.
Saturday 10th June, 1770
Wind lifting N.N.E. Briefly delegated captaining duties to Quartermaster Evans following suggestion for

greater democracy. Official ceremony ashore. Goodwill dominated.
Sunday 11th June, 1770
Wrote full and frank report for Captain Cook.'

There was a knock on the door and I put Hicks' report aside. Gastro poked his head around and peered in. When he saw that I was awake, he asked if I'd like a cup of tea. I nodded and he brought it in.

"Good to see you back on your feet," he said.

"I'm not, but I appreciate the sentiment. How did you get that lump on your forehead?"

"A coconut."

"That'll teach you to be more careful when you walk under trees. Put the tea near the lantern and close the door on your way out."

Smoothing the blankets around me, I reached for the tea and sipped. The warm sweetness tickled its way down my throat and settled in my stomach. Although I'd felt the sensation a thousand times before, this was the first time that I was fully conscious of it. The satisfaction was immense.

Monkhouse's report had fallen to the floor, so I put the empty cup back, leaned out of bed and picked the papers up. As I began reading, I noticed a more comprehensive detailing had been supplied.

'SURGEON'S REPORT
H.M.S. ENDEAVOUR
June 11, 1770
The following is a report of events that occurred on June 9, 10 and 11. Due to Captain Cook's indisposition, 2nd Lieutenant Hicks assumed command.

June 9; a.m. Private John Bowles and Sailmaker Ravenhill came down with chronic dysentery. Lt Hicks had them isolated ashore in a makeshift infirmary. He placed the men under my care. Tupia also fell ill and joined the other two.

June 9; p.m. Lt Hicks visited infirmary. Asked me what treatment I was giving Bowles and Ravenhill. I said a dysentery potion to relieve the intestinal spasms and a small brush to scrub the infected rectal area. I said that both men's expressed aim was to continue serving King George when recovered. Lt Hicks then questioned Tupia about his illness. Tupia said he had a sore throat. Lt Hicks then asked Tupia about his aim. Tupia said, 'To serve Kinky George and to get to small brush before Mr Ravenmad and upset Bowels!' Ravenhill threw the brush into Tupia's head. Bowles left his bed and rubbed his potion into Tupia's hair. Tupia screamed. I told the three infirmed to be quiet. Lt Hicks called me a 'medico of the mallard variety'. I yelled at Lt Hicks. The three infirmed yelled at Lt Hicks. Lt Hicks yelled at the three infirmed. Tupia threw a pillow and knocked down the tent pole. Tent collapsed. Lt Hicks knocked flat. Lt Hicks crawled out from under the canvas and left.

June 9; Late evening. Infirmed returned to ship in yawl and isolated in hold.

June 10; a.m. Lt Hicks appeared on deck wearing Captain Cook's hat. Announced that someone had suggested the practice of greater democratic participation. Informed the crew that suggestion was to be adopted. Declared that Quartermaster Evans was to be promoted to captain for a short period under Lt Hicks' supervision.

June 10; 1.30 p.m. Official *Occasion of Appointment* held ashore. Carpenter Satterley had built partially-enclosed stage just back from beach. Crew lined up in front of stage.

June 10; 2 p.m. Evans escorted from ship in long-boat and waited behind pine tree until introduced. Lt Hicks walked onto the stage and said, 'This is a swearing-in ceremony for our captain designate, Mr Evans.' Evans walked in and the crew let loose with a barrage of expletives such as 'beard splitter', 'lobcock', 'flapdoodle' and 'swag-bellied maggot pie'. Evans announced that everyone was going to be lashed. Master Molyneux called Captain Designate Evans a despot. Seaman Peckover shouted back that Evans was a teetotaller. Molyneux punched Peckover in the nasopharynx region and yelled, 'The word was *despot*, not pisspot.' Molyneux and Peckover screamed at each other like fish-hawkers at the Billingsgate market. Seaman Dozey threw a coconut at Gastro's head, causing a minor contusion. Gastro threw an artichoke at Tupia which resulted in major confusion. Tupia threw a tantrum. Sgt Edgecumbe fired a volley of shot into the air. Crew fell flat onto the stage. Stage collapsed. Lt Hicks knocked flat. Lt Hicks crawled out from under the debris and left ceremony.

June 10: Late evening. Crew returned to ship in long-boat and confined to quarters.

June 11: a.m. Captain Designate Evans appeared on deck wearing Captain Cook's hat. Sgt Edgecumbe was with him, lash in hand. Crew was quiet.

June 11: Early evening. Attended Captain Cook. The prognosis was positive. He ate a little food. We talked.

He asked me to write this report. I left with Lt Hicks. Lt Hicks asked me not to write this report.'

As I placed Monkhouse's report on top of Hicks', I almost heard myself groan under the weight of the contradictions. If Hicks' was factual, then all was well. If Monkhouse's contained the truth, which seemed likely given its final sentence, then Banks had any number of highwaymen to choose from when he finally decided to steal control of the *Endeavour*. And if that moment was imminent, what resistance could I put up, given my condition?

The time for languishing in bed was over, so I pushed off the blanket, put my feet on the floor and walked slowly over to the window. A brisk and salty sou'easterly stung my eyes, banishing the sleep and bringing my senses to life. All about, the sky glowed with an orange so warm and soft that I could almost taste its sweetness. And across the water to starboard, the moon's clear reflection was a scribble of gold on blue. More contrasts and contradictions. With a huge gulp, I took Nature's breath into my lungs and once again considered whose report was more likely to be accurate. Then, unexpectedly, help was provided. It came by way of the voices that filtered in from the main deck above the window. The first belonged to Quartermaster Evans, the captain designate.

"Evenin', Lieutenant."

The voice that replied, "And good evening to you," was Hicks'.

"Nice night, Lieutenant."

"Indeed, Captain Evans. Congratulations on the job you've done so far but can I make a couple of suggestions?"

"No. Fuck off or I'll have you flogged."

"You can't have me flogged!"

"Yes I can. You made me cap'n and a cap'n can have anyone flogged."

"Evans, I'll have you flogged for threatening to have me flogged!"

"Yeah? Then if you're threatenin' to have me flogged because I threatened to have you flogged, then I'll have you feckin' flogged for threatenin' to have me friggin' flogged! Is that clear?"

"What's clear is that you've flipped your fat lid. Now just shut up and listen. To avoid the danger of running into one of the islands, you'd better shorten sail and haul off shore east-north-east."

"I was goin' t'do that anyway."

"Good. When was the last time you ordered a sounding?"

"Ten minutes ago."

"And the depth of the water?"

"I don't know. Ask Ponto and Gathrey. They're out in the pinny about a hundred yards astern."

"That's *pinnace*, and why are they astern? What's the point in sounding water that we've already sailed over? They should be a hundred yards forward of the bow."

"They were, but we caught up with 'em."

As I was silently berating myself for being too weak to go atop, I felt the vibrations of heavy footsteps and heard another voice. It was John Gore's. "Evening, gentlemen. Any trouble, Captain Evans?"

"No. Mr Hicks was just congratulatin' me on the job I've been doin'. You know, orderin' soundin's and takin' lessons from Dozey on how to calculate our position."

"Which is?"

"Well, I'm standin' here next to the wheel, you're standin' next to me with your big flat feet on top of mine and Mr Hicks is about an inch away from my throat with his bare face hangin' out. How's that for a sharp eye?"

"Just keep it focused on our course."

At Hicks' mention of our course, I tried to move away from the window but my legs gave out. However, the notion that Monkhouse's report was the more accurate was strengthening with each word that Hicks then uttered.

"And speaking of our course, that reminds me of the second suggestion I was going to make. You'd find it easier to control the ship if you took your hands out of your pockets and put them on the wheel. That's it. Now turn it to port. No, that's starboard. Don't you know the difference between port and starboard?"

"Port's right and starboard's left, right?"

"No, port's left and starboard's right. Gore, am I right or wrong?"

"That depends on where you're standing," Gore observed. "If you're looking from the stern to the bow, then port's left and starboard's right. Sorry, that's wrong. Looking from the stern, starboard's left and port's right. But if I'm wrong, and port's left looking from the stern, then that makes you right and Evans wrong. Evans, is that right?"

"I couldn't have said it any fuckin' clearer meself."

I don't know what Hicks did to Evans at that moment, but it was sufficiently energetic to make Gore cry out, "Leave him alone! You're carrying on as if our lives depended on this."

"It might just bloody-well come to that. Evans, get your hands back on that wheel and turn it. Not so hard. That's better, but less wrist. No, I said 'less', not *left*. Don't jerk it! Steady, you've spun it too far! Turn it the other way, you stupid bastard!"

"Stop shoutin'! You're confusin' me! Which friggin' way do you want me to turn it?"

"Stort! No, hard to parboard, quick! Not that quick! Gore, you gutless shag-bag! Get yourself out of the long-boat and grab this bloody wheel off him! Evans, get your frigging feet off it!"

"They're not *my* friggin' feet!"

"Gore, will you stand up! Evans, turn it back! Look out, you'll have us on those bloody rocks!"

"Piss off, Hicks! The friggin' rocks are miles away!"

"Evans, you sharp-eyed muck snipe, turn the bloody telescope around the other way!"

"Shit, you're right for once! Molyneux! Tack or heave-away or throw up or whatever but just get us the fuck out of here!"

The sound that followed was horrendous; a scraping so loud and long that it reverberated throughout the entire ship for more than a minute. Monday the 11th of June, 1770. 10.54 p.m.. The *Endeavour* was stuck fast on a reef.

I was immobilised for only a few seconds before an energising fear stiffened my knees and braced my arms. With no time to dress properly, I simply pulled on my trousers, buttoned my coat and hurried as best I could from the cabin.

And then it struck me; a tide of human hysteria, washing backwards and forwards, so lost to reason that it almost swept me off my feet. Hands pushing, legs kicking, feet running. Cowards trampling on thieves treading on idlers. Foul words renting the air; even fouler tempers raging in the clamminess. The ragtag and bobtail that had shared my ship for the past two years now sharing in the headlong rush for self-preservation.

There was no point in trying to calm the rioters, so I squeezed back into my cabin and waited till the clamour had passed. When silence finally settled, I came out and made my way along the lower deck. From below, I could hear the sound of water as it gushed into the hold. It was a dreadful noise, cold and constant, thrusting against the planks as I stepped around the debris of strewn hammocks, shoes, cooking pots and smashed lanterns. Their oil spread across the timbers under my bare feet, anointing my soles and making sure steps impossible. Finally, after seconds that seemed like centuries, I reached the companionway, grabbed hold of the handrails and pulled myself up through the hatch.

And there it was again, the same rampage. Evans was sprawled beside the wheel, his legs tangled in the spokes and his hands in his pockets. As he tried to right himself, he screamed, "It's the cap'n's duty to go down with the ship so who wants to wear Jim's hat?"

As my head swivelled from the bow to the stern, with my mind struggling to apprehend the chaos, Richard Orton fell in a heap at my feet. He looked up at me, begged for a fortifier then disappeared under an avalanche of whirling limbs. Striding purposefully up onto the quarter-deck, I stood tall and waited. Along the deck, the ruckus continued, then Dozey caught my eye and stopped dead in his tracks. One or two others then noticed me, nudged several more, who in turn whispered and pointed, and before two minutes had passed, the entire crew was silent.

"Sergeant Edgecumbe," I said coldly. "Arrest any man who so much as blinks. If he resists, shoot him."

I was fully aware of the consequences inherent in the order, but at that moment there was only one thing on my mind; if our ship and our lives were to be saved, then co-operation was vital. And if the point of a musket was necessary to achieve that co-operation, then so be it. Fortunately, nobody dissented, so I said, "Keep it that way and we just might survive the night."

Buttoning my coat all the way to the collar, I then instructed Mr Gore to organise a pumping party. As the men assigned worked desperately in the hold to keep our stricken vessel afloat, I ordered Gathrey to lower the sails so that they couldn't drive the keel further along the coral.

"And when you've done that, hoist out the boats! I want the stream anchor slung beneath the long-boat and placed as far astern as you can. Then come back and take both bowers out on the longest possible cables. One to the starboard quarter and the other right astern. And take care to secure them. When the tide makes again, I want to be able to haul the ship off!"

"Aye aye, Captain!"

"Master Molyneux! Give me a sounding!"

"Under the larboard bow where the ship struck we've only got four feet!"

"Thank you. Master's Mate Pickersgill! Take Ponto and half a dozen others aloft on all three masts and send down the topgallant and topsail yards. When that's done, send down both the topgallant and topmasts and lash them in the water alongside. I want this ship stripped as far as she'll go!"

"Right, Sir!"

Through the long, moonlit night the men worked, pumping out the water and throwing overboard everything of weight; six guns, their carriages, iron and stone ballast, jars, stores, casks and hoops. It was arduous work, but at least it was honest.

As morning shed its encouraging warmth and light upon the waters surrounding the *Endeavour*, the full effect of the men's labours became glaringly apparent. Our once proud ship now sat like a hulk in water a foot less than when she had originally struck. No amount of heaving on all the anchors would move her and with land being more than twenty miles away, our circumstances looked desperate. Was it any wonder that I called the north point of land *Cape Tribulation*? For a day we waited, exhausted and fearing the worst. Barely able to move a muscle, the men rested in the sun on the deck, occasionally stirring to sip water or nibble some meagre sustenance. Some prayed quietly under the glare of the Cyclops sun, while one or two others hummed melodies that were a reminder of home. If they were to ever see it again, my experience, their work, Providence and a degree of luck would need to combine at just the right moment.

The imminent high water was the only chance the ship had of floating, and with the leaks in the hold increasing, the pumps could barely contain the flood. And if high water failed to shift her, then the inevitable would occur; the *Endeavour*, home to so many sailors for so many long and lonely months, would sink. And with her, our hopes.

Under another burnished twilight sky, we held our breaths as the tide reached its peak. There was a slight rolling as the hull responded to the increase in water and then, like the burden of a condemned prisoner pardoned at the last moment, the *Endeavour* lifted free of her fate and floated. And with her our joy. However, it needed to be tempered because the task was only half done. The ship still needed to be pulled from the reef, but was the water deep enough? I was faced with a dilemma. Should I leave her where she lay, floating but in danger of being pushed back and smashed on the coral, or should I attempt to heave her off in waters that might still harbour hidden dangers?

"Master Molyneux! Give me a sounding!"

"Three and a half feet in the hold!"

I gave the only order possible. "Heave her off!"

Like a bull being pulled free from a bog, the *Endeavour* began to inch her way forward, the cable on the stream anchor stretched tight and the muscles of the men working the windlass and capstan stretched even tighter.

"She's off and floating!" shouted the boatswain ahead in the long-boat. "We've done it!"

At that moment, the men's anxiety transformed itself into euphoria and they attended the pumps with renewed vigour and shouts of relief.

Such was their enthusiasm that by 8 the following morning, they'd gained considerably upon the leak. Masts and spars were then quickly rigged, and at close to 11, with a light breeze at E.S.E., the ship finally got under sail. As a last precaution, I had Midshipman Monkhouse fother the hull in order to block the leak as much as possible.

Like every other man who had worked so diligently for our recovery, I was completely exhausted. There was, however, an added factor specific to me; the responsibility of command. During the crisis, I had made decisions which, if incorrect, could have brought about catastrophe. Fortunately, they'd been sound, not only bringing about the ship's salvaging but also uniting the crew towards a positive, common purpose. Every man for himself had given way to all for one. This was the real achievement.

For the next few days we continued gently under sail, edging in for the land. I was constantly on the quarter-deck, supervising the navigation and prompting the masthead lookouts to watch for a shelter where we could repair the damage. Then, on the afternoon of June the 18th, we located a safe harbour. It was at the mouth of the waterway I named the *Endeavour River*, and here we warped the ship in and moored her alongside a steep beach. All the anchors, cables and hawsers were brought ashore and two tents erected, one for the sick, the other for the provisions. The emptying of the hold followed, and after a cannon had been slung from the main yard in order to keep her heeled to port at high water, the carpenters and I inspected the damage. Part of the sheathing from the larboard bow was lost, as was a section of the false keel, but the main leak was located on the floor timbers. It was here that the rocks had penetrated, cutting and tearing several holes. It was a chilling sight. Then, upon closer inspection, I noticed something truly remarkable. A large piece of coral was lodged in the biggest of the holes. Was it Providence or luck? Only personal belief could supply the answer. However, one aspect that was obvious to all was the irony; the reef which had threatened our lives had also saved them.

I immediately ordered the crew to assemble within the perimeter of the camp and told them about the coral. Some clapped and cheered while others shook hands. The same unity was evident during the next few days as they all worked feverishly towards the ship's rectification. This was even more remarkable because, as punishment for their lack of discipline just prior to, and during, the calamity off *Cape Tribulation*, all liberties had ceased; no rum, beer or unauthorised movement.

Although I was busy organising each day's activities, a distracting uncertainty played at the back of my mind; when would Banks strike? The time was both right and wrong; right because I hadn't fully recovered from my fever, and could therefore offer less resistance than normal; wrong because I'd saved the men's lives. Yet if that was my uncertainty, it was also Banks' dilemma. Should he strike now or wait, hoping for more trouble? The men were with me, but if more strife arose, then harsh punishment would descend, and a bitter seaman could easily turn to betrayal. There was little I could do about the situation, so I simply kept the men fully occupied with work.

The 30th of the month saw me and Carpenter Satterley beside the *Endeavour* at low water. It was close to midnight, and the damaged section was ablaze with the light from more than a dozen lanterns. Behind us were tall trees, silhouettes against the wall of cold, ebony air. Their canopies sheltered grey possums whose eyes glowed like small embers. The sight and mood were completely lost on Satterley, so I bent down beside him and saw that the repairs to the ship's bottom were almost complete.

"Most of it looks sound," I said, "but why have you jammed that cork into the largest hole?"

Satterley peered at his handiwork and replied, "It's the stopper I shoved in to keep the water out."

This was carpentry at its most incompetent and I told Satterley as much. He was crestfallen.

"Forget the self-pity," I continued, "and listen. The cork has to go. You've obviously wedged it in tightly so you'll need some sort of drilling tool. Have you got one?"

"I haven't, but Carpenter's Mate Hughes has. And he's had lots of experience with it."

"That's good because I don't want you anywhere near the hull from now on." I then called for Hughes and he came promptly.

"What's up, Sir?"

"Most of that cork."

"What do you want me to do?"

"The job Satterley should have done. Before new planks can be nailed to this area, his own damage has to be rectified. Fetch your special boring tool and get that stopper out now."

And that was the way the month of June ended, not with a bung but a wimbler.

A Plot Writ Large

For almost two months we stayed at the mouth of the *Endeavour River*, repairing the ship and gathering fresh water and provisions; cockles, clams, fish, turtles and palm cabbages. Inland hunts gave us wild pigs and kangaroos. They also gave the men a sporting release from their routine labour. We engaged the local natives only once during this period. The incident involved some minor pilfering of carpentry equipment which we got back in exchange for a small mirror and five of Banks' specimen jars. The natives were so pleased with their trinkets that they regularly supplied us with even more fresh food. They also showed Banks how to hunt kangaroos with a curved stick they called a 'boomerang', but the only things he succeeded in wounding were his upper-class pride and his reputation as a skilled marksman. In fact, the implement only returned after Banks threw it then sent his whippet out to fetch it. With friendliness dominating our encampment, I began to harbour hopes that the same mood might prevail during our voyage home.

So, on the morning of August the 4th, with the ship finally repaired and fully provisioned, I gave the order that every man had been waiting for; "Warp her out!" A light air from the land saw us get under sail and we moved out gently. With a man ahead sounding and Pickersgill stationed in the masthead lookout, we eased our way through the shoals. This practice was maintained for several days, and just when I thought our passage to open sea was clear, calamity almost struck again.

On the morning of the 16th, after charting our previous day's course, I came on deck and noticed Quartermaster Evans in the lookout attempting to find a safe channel through the reef that had earlier claimed us. We were three or four miles from the line of coral when, suddenly, the wind dropped and we were carried on a swell towards the jagged shelf. A mountainous surf was only a few hundred yards in front. Lieutenant Hicks, almost panic-stricken at the helm, couldn't decide which course to steer, so he shouted to Evans, "Port or starboard?"

"That depends which way you're lookin'!" Evans yelled down, his reply almost drowned out by the crash and fury of the breakers.

The words, like the waves with their beckoning, foamy fingers, were chillingly familiar, and if I'd allowed the conversation to proceed as it had earlier, so, too, would have the ship. Neither disaster was going to happen again, I resolved, so I ordered Hicks to turn half a degree starboard. He swung the wheel in the nick of time and the *Endeavour* squeezed through a gap in the reef that had no more than two inches of clearance on either side. Seven days later we rounded the northern extremity of land, *Cape York*, slipped free of the labyrinth through the passage I called the *Endeavour Straight*, and sailed west towards New Guinea. A commission completed. History made. But only just.

As I stood on the quarter-deck under a sky as blue and wide as the water that deepened with every wave crested, I knew that the world was mine and that it could no longer surprise me. Then, like Achilles, the heel of my certainty was wounded by the sharp realisation of something overlooked; the treacherous reef lurking in the waters of my own life. And then I saw him, from the corner of my eye, talking with Charles Green and Able Seaman Matthews as the three of them huddled at the bow. Matthews had been reprimanded a week earlier for breeding more 'field-mice', so it came as no surprise to see Banks actively pursuing his company. As they whispered behind their hands, Green kept looking around to make sure they weren't being overheard. Just as the ship slipped into a hollow between two large swells, Edgecumbe joined the group. He was carrying a musket, which of itself was not alarming as I'd ordered him to be constantly armed as a bulwark against the resurfacing of behaviour not befitting sailors in the King's service.

With *Cape York* now a speck astern, I began to feel apprehensive. When Banks then pointed and started walking towards me with the burly sergeant only a step behind, my heart actually skipped a beat. This was the encounter I'd been dreading, yet at that moment my fear left and a surge of furious energy flowed in. Not waiting to be kissed on the cheek in exchange for thirty pieces of Banks' silver, I threw back my shoulders and strode forward. In the furnace of the midday heat, Edgecumbe wilted under the intensity of my resolve and judiciously placed his firearm behind the wheel. My attention was now fully focused on Banks and we met in the centre of the deck. Face to face. My one, his two.

"So," I said calmly, my pacific tone in contrast to the Atlantic tempest of my gaze, "the time has come. Do what you must."

The contemptible cur took a white silk handkerchief from his waistcoat pocket and wiped his sweating hands. A cough followed. He seemed hesitant. His courage was found wanting. Mine wasn't, so I sought to cower him further by striking first.

"All right, you hen-hearted little lobcock, I'll make it easier for you. It was my decision to place Hicks in charge when I was forced to bed with fever. As a result, we almost lost our lives on the reef. I'll also concede that certain people have caused trouble. As these things occurred on my ship, I take full responsibility. If you now want to seize both, Edgecumbe will have to pull that trigger first."

Banks just stood there, weighing my words. He turned to Edgecumbe, then looked back at me.

"What are you talking about?"

His toying was intolerable. "You're a grown man, Banks, so don't play games."

The botanist again looked at his accomplice and said, "Is this making any sense to you?"

Edgecumbe shook his head. At that moment the sun could have disappeared without any appreciable loss of heat because I was boiling. Swinging my fist up, I thumped the mainmast and told Banks that his actions hadn't caught me by surprise because I'd had him pegged as a mutineer since April. The botanist jumped back in fear and knocked Edgecumbe flat.

"Me, a mutineer? That's ridiculous! Who put that idea into your head?"

I took a step nearer to the plotter and hissed between gritted teeth, "You did! Gore found your notes and showed me."

Banks held his head then threw up his hands. "The notes! *Now* I understand why you've been behaving so strangely!" He then smoothed the furrow from his brow and said, "Let's walk around the deck. There's something I need to tell you."

The *Endeavour's* bow rose and fell and drove on as we began our stroll.

"James," the botanist said as his feet moved in unison with mine, "the reason I was coming to talk to you was because the men wanted me to formally thank you for the sterling job you did in saving our lives."

I walked on and said nothing.

"And let me assure you I haven't been planning any overthrow. The paper you read that mentioned 'mutiny' and 'plot' was simply a summary I jotted down regarding the novel I'm writing. You know, characters and setting? Originally it was about a tyrannical captain at odds with his reasonable crew on a long sea voyage."

I stopped, grabbed the handrails for support and looked Joseph squarely in the eye. "A novel? More like a novel excuse."

"It's the truth, James. I'm putting a book together."

"Mr Banks," I said with undisguised contempt, "you couldn't put Orton and a bottle of rum together with any measure of success. If this book business is true, then explain the part in your notes that said you were the only one who could carry it out successfully?"

"Who else could write *my* novel?"

"What about the time I saw you and Green in the magazine? Do you deny that you were asking him to check your plans to see that nothing was overlooked?"

Banks raised his eyebrows ruefully and, with his mood building to a panshard, protested, "What sort of contemptible hugger-mugger do you think I am?"

"For your sake, I'll assume that was a rhetorical question, but I still want an answer to mine."

"I was simply asking Mr Green to collaborate with me on a few details, but he wasn't keen because he incorrectly envisioned the book to be a critical disaster."

"And who said Green wasn't a natural observer?"

"What was that?"

"I said Green was by nature reserved."

Banks nodded. "He might see it differently now that I've changed the plot and main character. The captain's a fair-minded gentleman but his crew's ungovernable. Once it's in print, it'll sell like buns in Chelsea."

I was still dubious. "You had Matthews' ear a while ago. What's his involvement?"

I fell in beside Banks as he started strolling again. "He's a reasonable writer himself, having done the 'Happy Birthday' sign for Hicks' party, so I asked him to run his quill through the odd spelling error."

"But you couldn't have seen the sign because you weren't at the party."

"That's right. I told Mr Gore I had something more important to do in my cabin. It was the book. You can't say no to the muse when she sits on your face."

"You're confused. It's 'shoulder', not 'face'."

"No, *you're* confused. I'm Joseph Banks, not John Bunyan."

Having nailed on most of the boards, the hull of Banks' story now appeared as a more solid construction. However, it still needed two crucial planks to keep it from sinking. The first was Charles Green's explanation and I demanded to hear it. Charles responded quickly to the botanist's beckoning hand and wasted no time in confirming the story.

The second was as tangible as wood itself. "If you *are* writing a book," I said, "go and fetch it."

"If it'll put your mind at ease," Banks replied as he stepped down through the hatch. Five minutes later he returned with a bundle of papers and handed them to me. His eyes were wide with excited anticipation.

"Perhaps I've misjudged you," I conceded, "but let me skim through, just to make sure."

Banks buffed his boots on the backs of his trousers then smiled like a teacher's pet waiting to receive his report card. I turned to the title page and his book was laid bare.

'THE INCREDIBLY YOUNG MAN AND THE SEA
A Novel by Joseph Banks Esq
Edited by Able Seaman Thomas Matthews

CHAPTER 1
It had been a dark and stormy night but now it was a bright and sunny day. The water was as flat as a pancake and it was blue and wet. The water was, not the pancake. Pancakes are yellow. Except when Gastro cooks them. They're green because of the bloody artichokes he chucks in them. Anyway, Admiral Josephus Bonks, the youngest admiral ever in the entire history of the British navy, stood proudly on the deck of his ship H.M.S Enema with 2nd Lieutenant Zachariah Slackhips. Suddenly, Lieutenant Slackhips looked starboard and shouted, "Land ho!"

Then the lookout asked, "Admiral Bonks, when do you think we will be leaving the dock to start our astonishing journey?"

Admiral Bonks replied, "Lift up the anchor? ~~ANgka Ankar WANKER~~ MEtaL FiNG and we'll start now."

Then the admiral went down to his cabin and started reading some difficult? ~~DIFycul Duffelcoat~~ HArD botany books because he'd been to Oxford University and he was a Fellow? ~~maN chaP~~ ToFF of the Royal Society.

A few months later, the ship sailed into an unbelievably calm harbour of smooth water near Otaheite. While it was there, all the crewmen played fast and loose with the native girls but Admiral Bonks didn't. He was chaste? CHAfFeD and wanted to save himself for marriage.

It was incredibly dark at night when they finally left the harbour after being there and when they reached open water it was amazingly rough. The sea's like that in that neck of the woods.

CHAPTER 2

Some months later, a thickhead named Fourby Two expired? ~~pissed aWay Dyde~~ CRoakEd while eating dinner. No-one went back for seconds that night. Then some natives kidnapped the cook and held him for ransom. The crew raised 25 pounds and 3rd Lieutenant Cork said to the natives, "We'll double it if you keep the maggot-boiling looby."

CHAPTER 3

After Admiral Bonks had discovered a missing continent of land that was not found by him before he saw it, a beef-witted navy sailor named Quartermaster Evans? ~~KWarta KINKYMaste WaTERmelo whataBASTARD~~ MiStER EVanS crashed the ship into a reef. Everyone got scared except the admiral. He took control and saved the men's lives. Then all the men had big smiles and huge grins? GRoiNs and they cheered because they loved Admiral Bonks because he was fantastically brave and handsome.

CHAPTER 4
When the voyage was over, Admiral Bonks sailed home to England. Thousands of people swam out to greet him as he heroically rowed his ship up the Thames. Waiting for him on the dock were 500 women who loved him. They weren't tuppeny tarts or sixpenny strumpets because Admiral Bonks, like all men of superior position, only carried folding money.
The next day, the King made Admiral Bonks a Knight of the Realm and his incredibly popular book sold over a million copies in just three...'

My eyes were still rapidly moving backwards and forwards as I looked up from the page. I paused before speaking, searching for the right words. "Joseph, it's a real piece of work."

Banks smiled self-effacingly.

"And I see you've included the chaotic flow we talked about some months ago."

"You mean the 'Sewer-pipe of Consciousness' technique?"

"I thought we'd settle on 'stream' but given what I've just read, 'sewer-pipe' is apposite."

The heat was now scorching, so Banks took off his jacket and casually draped it over the windlass. "Of course, that's just the first draft, so it might need some minor revision but I'm sure I've got the body of the thing dead right."

After months of mayhem and wearying miles sailed abreast of a challenging coast, the temptation to unleash my tongue upon the ludibrious botanist was too strong to resist. "Give it two weeks and it'll be fully decomposed."

"Sorry, James, I missed that because of those gulls squawking on the poop rail."

"I said, 'Give it a few tweaks and it'll be beautifully composed'. And when the crew reads it, they'll be speechless."

At the mention of the men, Joseph smiled. "Why deprive them of pleasure by waiting a month? I want to read what I've done to them today. An artist's work has the power to change men's lives."

So near to 9 that night, with the crew crowded along the lantern-lit lower deck, Joseph read his piece of work aloud. I'd anticipated the response correctly, so I waited till he'd left, then said, "Listen carefully, you putrid parade of guts and garbage. If I have the slightest trouble from anyone between here and England, I'll ask Banks to read out more of his stuff."

Almost twelve months later, I wrote the final entry in the *Endeavour's* log;

'**THURSDAY 18th July 1771**. Clear, serene weather. Sailed up the Thames in the a.m.. Docked at Galleon's

Reach. Pleased to report that since leaving the Great Southern Continent, the entire crew has behaved in exemplary fashion, due solely to the life-changing work of Joseph Banks.

James Cook
H.M.S. *Endeavour*'

Lightning Source UK Ltd.
Milton Keynes UK
UKHW020809160921
390679UK00003B/212